THE GIRL IN THE SNOW

ALEXANDRIA CLARKE

Copyright 2020 All rights reserved worldwide. No part of this document may be reproduced or transmitted in any form, by any means without prior written permission, except for brief excerpts in reviews or analysis.

❦ Created with Vellum

1

Raising kids was like maintaining a garden. Some days, your plants thrived and smiled up at the sun, and radiant warmth filled your soul as your pride blossomed. You watered and fed them. You provided them with an enriching environment to grow in. You poured your heart into their wellness with the hope it would come back to you tenfold.

Other days, your plants shriveled up. They cried and threw temper tantrums. They refused to set the table or get dressed. Your hyperactive bird of paradise got detention for the third time this week and your diabetic succulent forgot to reload the cartridge for his insulin pump, so you had to leave work early and rush to deliver it to his middle school.

Oh, wait. Those were my kids.

"Do you have it?" I asked the eighth time that morning.

Benji, my seven year old, zoomed past me, dressed head-to-toe in bright orange. He'd chosen the snow jacket and pants for himself, and I'd secretly rejoiced. It would be easy to spot him on the slopes at Wolf Park, our favorite ski spot in North Carolina.

"Can we go yet?" he whined, tugging on my shirt. No answer to my question.

In the bathroom, I checked my bag of toiletries again. Deodorant, contact lens solution, Mommy's "special pills," also known as my anti-anxiety medication. All there. I zipped the bag shut and tossed it into my suitcase.

"In a minute," I told Benji. "Do you have your insulin?"

Benji hopped on the balls of his feet. Sometimes, I couldn't tell if he was excited or really needed to go to the bathroom. His one-track mind couldn't process my question while he gyrated. "You said 'in a minute' fifteen minutes ago."

I ran a comb through my hair, wishing I'd had time to get it cut and styled before our annual trip to the mountains. "Just making sure we have everything we need. Like your insulin."

"For God's sake," a lazy voice echoed behind me.

My thirteen year old, Ophelia, slouched into the bathroom. Her heavily-lidded eyes blinked blearily at me in the mirror. "*I packed Benji's insulin. Can we go or what? I'm bored.*"

I tossed her the keys. "Warm up the car. Don't touch the pedals. I don't want a repeat of last time."

Ophelia lumbered off, muttering, "It was an *accident.*"

Ophelia's "accident" had caused my new SUV to roll backward out of the driveway and pulverize the neighbor's mailbox across the street. Several hundred dollars later, the neighbor had a new mailbox, but my bumper still bore marks from the incident.

Sweat shone on Benji's face. I unzipped the collar of his jacket. "You're going to overheat, buddy. It takes an hour to get there. You don't have to wear your snow jacket in the car."

Determined, he zipped the collar up to his chin. "I want to be ready for when we get there."

I ruffled his hair. Like me, he needed a trim. When his locks grew too long, they grew upward in thick curls. He was the spitting image of his father with bright blue eyes, olive skin, and a stout stature. Ophelia was the polar opposite. She was all legs, blonde hair, and brown eyes, like my side of the family. At least one of my kids looked related to me.

. . .

Downstairs, I glanced through the front window to make sure Ophelia hadn't taken the SUV for a joyride. She sat in the driver's seat, starting at her phone, as the car puffed exhaust. She hadn't bothered to de-ice the windshield.

"Ophelia!" I called from the front door.

She rolled down the window and stuck her head out. "What?"

"Scrape the windshield!"

"It's freezing outside!"

"Do you want to get to Wolf Park on time or not?"

Rolling her eyes, she made a show of getting out of the car. I watched until she retrieved the ice scraper from the glove box and started the job. Then I went into the kitchen to round up some snacks. When Benji tanked without warning, peanut butter and rice cakes perked him right up. I tossed Ophelia's favorite protein bars into a reusable grocery bag with Benji's things and made to put the snacks with the other items that needed to go in the car.

As I stepped backward, I tripped over Benji, who'd been tailing me like a lost puppy since we left the bathroom. With a huff of air from my lungs, I landed hard on my tailbone. The bag of snacks flew out of my grasp.

"Sorry, Mom!" Benji knelt beside me, and his

jacket puffed up around his neck. "I didn't mean to trip you!"

"I know, buddy." I rubbed my throbbing butt and hoisted myself up. "Why don't you help me get the bags into the car?"

Benji dragged the largest suitcase through the front door. When he slipped on the icy sidewalk and almost broke a wrist, I relieved him of my baggage and handed him Ophelia's smaller duffel bag instead. He happily marched it to the trunk.

When I saw the windshield, I frowned. The sides were scraped clean, but a thin layer of ice still frosted the middle. Ophelia, in the passenger's seat, pretended not to notice I'd come out.

I opened the driver's door and tossed the bag of snacks into Ophelia's lap. "Hey, kid. That windshield job is not up to par. What am I paying you for?"

"You're not paying me," she said, eyes glued to her phone. "And I can't reach the middle."

I grabbed the ice scraper and pulled on the handle. "It extends. You know that."

She feigned innocence. "Does it?"

Sighing, I ducked out of the car to finish the job myself. The house's shadow loomed over me as I worked, and the cold set in quick. Once upon a time, our two-story home with the cute brick accents and cozy porch was my dream place to live. Now, it reminded me of all the things that had gone wrong in the last several years. Worst of all, I paid the mortgage by myself these days.

"You okay, Mom?" Benji asked as I got in the car and wedged the ice scraper next to Ophelia's feet.

"Tired," I replied. I jabbed my thumb at Ophelia. "You, in the back."

Her mouth dropped open. "Why?"

"You're too young to sit in the front."

"I'm thirteen!" She flung the sun shield down to read off the warning signs. "This says children younger than twelve!"

"We're going by my rules, not those."

"You mean the ones set by the vehicle manufacturer?" she growled.

"Exactly. Mom trumps vehicle manufacturer. In the back, please."

Grumbling under her breath, Ophelia crawled between the front seats, making sure to dangle her dirty sneakers in my face, and into the back. "Can't believe I have to sit with Benji like I'm seven."

"I'm almost eight," Benji reminded her triumphantly. "Plus I like sitting in the back. These chairs lean farther back." To demonstrate, he pulled the lever and reclined as far as possible. "Whoa! There we go."

"You're stupid," Ophelia said.

"Don't call your brother stupid," I scolded, backing carefully out of the driveway. "Benji, stop playing with the seat before you break the lever. Last call: does everyone have everything they need?"

"Yes," Benji said.

Ophelia groaned. "Yes, for God's sake."

"Stop saying that. Off we go."

Fifteen minutes later, as I merged onto the interstate, Ophelia said, "Oh, crap. Mom?"

"Yes, Ophelia?"

"I forgot the bag with Benji's insulin."

THE PHONE RANG over the Bluetooth speaker. I hit the answer button instinctively, thinking it might be about work, but when my mother's voice permeated the car, I regretted my hasty decision.

"Carolina, where are you?"

"We share a Google calendar, Mother. You know where I am."

Her scoff echoed through the car. I glanced in the mirror to check the kids' reactions. Ophelia had her headphones in. She likely couldn't hear her grandmother speaking. Benji listened with terse alertness.

"I don't know why you do it," my mother said. "An annual ski trip to see your ex-husband and his new family? It's masochistic."

"Amos and I are on good terms," I said. "We do this for the kids. They deserve a chance to see their dad."

"Face it, honey," she replied. "Just because he pays child support doesn't mean he cares about Benji and O."

In the back, Benji's lip wobbled. He reclined his seat all the way back and stared at the ceiling of the car.

"It's for the kids," I repeated, my argument waning.

"Do I need to remind you what happened between you and that dick you call an ex-husband?" she asked shrilly. "He forced you to quit your job then divorced you when you finally did."

"He didn't force me—"

"Carolina, don't bullshit me. I know what happened."

"The kids are in the car," I snapped. "They can hear you. I'll text you when we get there."

"Give Amos a smack for me."

"Bye, Mom." I hung up. "You okay, Benji?"

He lifted his head. "Do you think Dad's going to forget my birthday again?"

"No way, buddy!" I winced as another car passed me in the left lane and the driver gestured rudely to let me know I was going too slow for his taste. "Your dad probably has something amazing planned."

THE KIDS WERE quiet for the rest of the drive. After a

bathroom break for Benji and a snack break for Ophelia because I'd apparently packed the wrong protein bars, we arrived at Wolf Park an hour and a half later.

Six years ago, when I was working for the FBI, I hadn't had any trouble affording five days' vacation at Wolf Park. Ever since I retired from the agency to focus on my marriage—an action that had backfired—I scrounged to cobble together the funds for one small room at the luxury ski resort. Teaching criminology at a local community college didn't pay the bills like the agency did. Ophelia and Benji were lucky we could afford to go skiing this year at all.

Benji woke up from his nap, as if he could sense our proximity to the mountain. He yanked his seatbelt loose and leaned through the front seats to get a better look at the main building.

The resort was an enormous puzzle of room windows and balconies. Steam from guests' private hot tubs rose in the air. Though it was after Christmas, holiday decorations hung from the streetlights that lined the circular driveway. In the distance, three separate chair lifts chugged up the mountain, depositing guests at the ski routes of their choosing.

Private cabins dotted the hillside, puffing chimney smoke into the air. When Amos and I were married, we rented a cabin every year for our trip. Things were different then. We had more money and less patience for each other. We spent most of our vacation yelling at each other in those cabins.

"Finally," Ophelia said, taking out her headphones at last. "That took forever."

I parked along the curb outside the lobby. Guests hurried by in thick jackets, their cheeks pink from the wind as they cheerfully carried snowboards and skis to and from the slopes. As a bellboy approached the car, I turned around to address my children.

"Listen up," I said. "You are both to be on your best behavior, understand? This is the first year Pilar and her daughters are with us, and you *will* treat them with respect."

Ophelia crossed her arms. "I am not hanging out with Marin. I don't care if we're the same age. She's pompous and annoying."

"Marin is well-spoken and polite. What a dream," I added dryly. "You will be nice to her *and* Nessa. Otherwise, you won't be able to ride the new bike you got from Christmas until July. Got it?"

Ophelia glared at me and stuck her headphones back in. The bell boy opened my door for me.

"Good afternoon, ma'am," he said. "Can I help you take your luggage inside while you head to the front desk?"

"That would be great. Thanks."

As the bell boy loaded the baggage onto a cart, I herded Ophelia and Benji into the lobby. A hundred-foot artificial Christmas tree towered in the resort's hub, reaching toward the upper floors. Decorations of silver and gold hung from its scentless branches. Matching garlands and baubles adorned the front desk. As I waited in line to check in, Ophelia and Benji climbed onto the stone pillars around the enormous tree and swatted at the lowest hanging fruit like trouble-making cats.

"Carolina?"

I turned toward the voice and spotted a willowy woman with flowing waves of black hair, beautifully cut cheekbones, and warm brown eyes. Two girls—fourteen and nine—held the woman's hands. They both looked exactly like their mother. My stomach flipped. I didn't expect to see my ex-husband's new wife and kids before I'd guzzled a few glasses of wine.

I arranged my face in a smile. "Hi, Pilar. Girls. Where's Amos?"

"He's renting equipment for the day."

Pilar hugged me, naturally comfortable with the affection. I stood stiffly, unsure of what to do, as she brushed her lips against my cheek. She presented her daughters.

"You remember Carolina. Right, girls?"

Nessa, the younger of the two, wrapped her arms around my waist. "Hi, Lina! It's nice to see you again."

Marin smiled politely. "Hi. Is Ophelia here?"

Right on cue, Ophelia knocked a glass bauble off the tree. The ornament shattered when it hit the floor. As a resort employee hurried over with a broom to sweep up the shards, Ophelia gave me a guilty look. Benji lifted his hands in a gesture of innocence.

"Get over here," I mouthed.

The kids came over.

"Say hi to Pilar and the girls," I ordered.

"Hi, Ophelia!" Marin said brightly, hugging my daughter. "I have so much to tell you about. Do you want to go skiing later?"

Ophelia kept her arms glued to her sides. "I don't ski."

"She snowboards," I supplied. "But you can still hit the slopes together."

"I like to go fast," Ophelia declared to Marin. "You'll have to keep up."

Marin looked down. "Oh, I'm a beginner."

Ophelia shrugged. "Too bad."

I gently seized the back of Ophelia's neck and steered her away from Marin. Benji shyly stepped forward and offered a piece of notebook paper to Nessa.

"It's a piping plover," he said, pointing to the bird he'd drawn in the car. "They remind me of you because they're small and round, like your cheeks."

Nessa's plump cheeks flushed as she accepted the drawing. "Thanks, Benji."

Benji scuffed his boot on the floor. "Hi, Pilar."

"Hi, Benji," she said softly. "That's a very good drawing."

My son beamed at her with pride he rarely afforded me. "It took me three hours to get all the details right."

Pilar clapped a hand to her heart. "My goodness! No wonder it's so beautiful." She looked up at me. "Are you staying in the cabins too? Maybe we're near each other. It's beautiful out there, isn't it? Amos said they've done renovations. Everything's brand new."

Heat crept up my neck. "We're in a room upstairs."

The front desk lady cleared her throat. "Ma'am? Are you ready to check in?"

Pilar put her arms around her daughters. "We'll let you three get settled. See you later?"

"Yes. Right. Of course."

They made their way across the lobby. Near the door, they joined a handsome man with dark curly hair like Benji's. As he smiled at Pilar, he caught sight of me over her shoulder. He nodded curtly. When Nessa took his hand, his happiness returned, and he led his new family outside.

"Ugh," Ophelia said. She had seen Amos, but Benji hadn't. "Dad was never that gooey with us."

I steered her toward the front desk. "Come on. Let's get to our room."

THE ROOM WAS tiny compared to the lush cabins. It featured one queen-sized bed and a pullout couch. Instead of a fully-equipped kitchen, it had a mini-fridge and a microwave oven. It smelled faintly musty, as if the last people to stay here had left their wet ski gear piled on the carpet.

"No balcony?" Benji said sadly, standing on his toes to see out of the window.

Ophelia joined him. "Great view of the parking lot though."

I set up the luggage rack and hauled my suitcase on top of it. "It's a nice room. Do you two know how lucky you are to be here? Most kids don't get ski vacations at all. You should learn to appreciate what you have."

"Blah, blah, blah." Ophelia dumped the entire contents of her duffel onto the couch. "I call the pull-out. Benji, you can share with Mom."

"What?" Benji cried. "I'm the man of the house, and it's my birthday! I should get the pull-out."

Ophelia snorted. "The *man* of the house? Give me a break. When you hit puberty, then we'll talk."

"Mom!" Benji protested.

I looked between my two kids, deciding which

battle to pick. "Sorry, Benj. Ophelia gets the pull-out."

Ophelia pumped her fist while Benji stomped his foot.

"That's not fair!"

"Ophelia kicks in her sleep," I said. "You don't. Do it for me, buddy?"

He frowned. "Fine."

"We don't have to go to dinner with *them*, do we?" Ophelia asked, lounging across her clothes. "Please say you won't torture me."

I started organizing Benji's clothes so we could find his things with ease. "We're here to spend time with your father, O. Of course we're going to dinner with them. Not tonight though. We agreed to give everyone time to settle in."

Ophelia moaned and dropped her head back. "This is going to be awful. There's no way I'm skiing with Marin, especially if she's slow. I don't do slow. I didn't come here to hang out on the bunny slope—"

"You came here because I told you to," I snapped with more ferocity than I intended.

Ophelia stared at me, dumbfounded by my sharp tone.

I took a deep breath. "Like I said, I need you both on your best behavior. Your father is married to Pilar. She's going to be in your lives from now on, as are Marin and Nessa. It's better if we all get along."

"I like Nessa," Benji said. "But she thinks I'm weird."

"No, she doesn't," I said.

"Yes, she does," Benji replied, unbothered. "I heard her say so."

Ophelia stood. "Let's go find her. I'm gonna punch her. No one gets to call you weird but me."

I seized Ophelia's shoulders. "Settle down, tiger. No one's punching anyone."

"She called your son weird," she said. "Are you going to take that?"

"I'm sure she didn't mean it." I directed her toward the pile of clothes on the couch. "Fold those and put them away so you have a place to sleep tonight." I checked my watch. "Are you two okay to be alone for ten minutes? I need to do something."

"I'm fine," Benji said.

Ophelia raised her eyebrows. "What do you need to do?"

"Parent stuff."

"You're meeting Dad?"

Benji's eyes widened. "You are? Can I come? I wanna see him!"

I gently pushed Benji onto the bed and tossed him the remote. "You'll see him tomorrow. Tonight is for grown-ups. Watch a movie or something, but don't pick one you have to pay for. My wallet's dried up."

Ophelia tackled Benji for control over the remote. As they wrestled, I checked my appearance in the mirror. My nicest sweater hung limply on my thin frame. The bags under my eyes found my tinted moisturizer for dominance. I had lipstick on my teeth. Furiously, I rubbed it off.

Ophelia appeared beside me. She kissed my cheek. "You look great, Mom."

"What? I don't care what I look like." I tucked my hair behind my ear. "We're already divorced anyway."

Ophelia gave me a knowing look.

"Stop it," I ordered. Shoving the room key in my pocket, I backed away from my daughter. "I'll be back in a few minutes."

She rolled her eyes. "Take your time."

AMOS SAT, his back straight, in the cigar lounge, a small bar tucked away in the quietest corner of the resort. Before we had the kids, we'd spent a lot of nights in this lounge, gazing at each other over two glasses of whiskey. My, how times had changed.

Amos glanced at me before I approached him, as if some instinct warned him of my coming. Like before, he nodded curtly. No wave or friendly smile. I crossed the bar and sat beside him.

"Vodka?" I asked, pointing to his clear drink. "That's not you."

"It's water." He leaned back to get a better look at me. "Something's different."

"My hair's longer."

"It's not that."

I flushed as his light eyes swept across my body and hoped the bar was dim enough to hide my imperfections. Surely he was comparing me to Pilar's immaculate form. "Anyway, how's work?"

"Fine. How are the kids?"

"You could call every once in a while and find out for yourself."

He wiped the condensation off the glass. "I thought we agreed not to fight."

"Did we?"

"It was an unspoken agreement."

I flagged the bartender and ordered a whiskey. "You're right. I told the kids to be nice to your new family. Guess I should take my own advice."

"Pilar is the kindest person I've ever met," Amos said. "Don't antagonize her."

"You never said that about me."

"I suppose that's why we're divorced."

I bit my cheek to keep my scathing reply in check. "Look, we're here so Ophelia and Benji can spend time with you. Please don't let them down."

Amos nodded. "And what about us?"

"We play nice," I offered. "We'll act cordial. Keep the conversation focused on the kids. I don't have a problem with Pilar or her girls. They're nice."

"They are nice," Amos agreed. He lifted his glass. "It's settled then. We'll be cordial."

I tapped my glass against his. "It's only five days, right?"

2

"Wake up, wake up, wake up!"

Benji jumped on the bed, his socked feet bouncing dangerously close to my torso. The mattress jiggled, and last night's whiskey gurgled in my stomach. I grabbed Benji's ankles and pulled. Unharmed, he landed on his butt and giggled madly.

"I'm up," I said, rubbing my bleary eyes. "What time is it?"

"Six-thirty."

"In the morning? Sheesh, dude, it didn't occur to you to let Mom sleep in on her vacation?"

Benji shook his head. "No way! We need to get breakfast and rent our boards and buy our ski passes and—"

Ophelia groaned loudly from the pull-out bed

and put a pillow over her ears. "Mom, can you put a muzzle on the puppy? Some of us are trying to sleep."

"Breakfast doesn't start until seven," I told Benji. "Your sister and I need some more time. Why don't you draw the view from the window if you're bored?"

Benji wrinkled his nose. "You want me to draw the parking lot?"

"You can see the mountains in the distance too."

"I don't do landscapes. I like birds and other animals."

"I know, buddy, but this is good practice."

He gazed longingly at his orange snow gear hanging in the closet. "Are you sure we can't go now?"

I tucked myself deeper beneath the blankets and closed my eyes again. "Half an hour, buddy. Then we'll head outside."

"Fine."

Benji crawled off the bed, marched over to the window, and yanked the curtains wide open, flooding the room with sunlight. Ophelia let out a war cry. Leaping from her bed, she tackled Benji and threw him backward in a wrestling move that belonged on NXT. Benji screamed, more out of surprise than injury, as Ophelia flipped him over and pinned him to the pull-out mattress.

"I'm sleeping!" she yelled, inches from his face.

I scrambled out from underneath the covers and attempted to wrench Ophelia off her brother. "Enough! Ophelia, let go of him!"

Ophelia relinquished her grasp and sat back with her teeth bared. "He shouldn't have opened the window like that!"

"Mom said I could!" Benji protested, rubbing his shoulders where Ophelia had restrained him. "I bruise easily! You should be grounded."

"What? You little punk—"

I grabbed Ophelia before she could lunge again. "Cool off," I ordered. "Your brother wasn't trying to annoy you."

She got back into bed and tugged the covers over her head, muttering, "He's always trying to annoy me."

"No, I'm not," Benji said.

"Yes, you are."

"No, I'm not."

"Yes, you—"

"Stop," I cut in, weary already. I drew the curtains together to block out most of the light but left a gap in the middle. "Ophelia, go back to bed. Benji, you can draw from here. Don't open the curtains any more. *Please,* both of you, be quiet."

As I crawled into bed, my phone rang. My mother's number showed up on screen. I almost didn't answer, but she was prone to incessant calling if she didn't get an immediate response.

"Well?" she demanded after I'd said hello. "Did Amos get ugly?"

Amos's intense eyes, strong jaw, and stout musculature flashed in my mind. He'd looked annoyingly handsome in the navy blue sweater he'd worn last night.

"He looks better than ever," I reported. "I suppose a happy marriage can have that effect on a person."

"Did he apologize for everything he did to you?"

I hid beneath the blankets and let the darkness comfort me. "Mom, it's been four years since we got divorced. We're trying to let it go and move on. I suggest you do the same."

"When he acknowledges the trouble he's caused you, I'll move on," she declared. "Or when you find a man better-looking and richer than Amos. That would show him."

"I appreciate your concern," I said impassively. "I'll work on securing a husband who will make Amos regret breaking up with me."

"You think I'm kidding, Carolina?"

"I know you're not."

She was quiet for a few seconds, a remarkable feat. "I called to make sure you're okay. I remember how upset you were after the divorce. Every time you see Amos, you come home in a terrible mood."

That was true. Whenever Amos and I had to meet up—to discuss custody, deal with finances, or hand over the kids—a soul-sucking pall came over me. At first, I blamed it on Amos, but I eventually realized the feeling stemmed from one thing: guilt.

My mother thought mine and Amos's divorce was his fault. She was wrong. I was the one who had royally screwed our marriage over. My previous job with the FBI was a huge commitment. I spent most of my time working on my case load. When I returned home in the evenings, I was too exhausted to care for my husband and children. Amos did the brunt of the housework. He took the kids to school, made their every meal, and helped them with their homework. He went to the parent-teacher meetings because I could never make it. He sacrificed his dream job for the sake of our family. I had dumped all our shared responsibilities on him and told myself my paycheck justified my lack of involvement.

Shortly after Benji turned two, Amos decided he couldn't do it anymore. He had given up too much for me. It was over.

Back then, I blamed everything on Amos. I called him sexist and misogynistic for not wanting to be a stay-at-home dad while I worked. I pretended his pride was the reason for our problems. In hindsight, I couldn't admit the truth, but it became clear when I had to juggle the kids and my new job without Amos's help for the first time ever.

My dignity prevented me from ever telling this to my mother, hence her continuing barrage of insults toward Amos.

"I'm doing better," I told Mom. "It's getting easier."

My dignity also prohibited me from telling my mother about the anti-anxiety medication I'd gotten from my primary care doctor. She was the type of woman who frowned upon drug use, pharmaceutical or not.

"I hope you're telling me the truth," she said. "If I think otherwise, I'm marching myself to Wolf Park and giving Amos a piece of my mind."

"Please don't," I replied. "That will only make it worse." I glanced at the clock. Fifteen minutes remained until Benji pounced on me for round two of his wake-up call. "Mom, I gotta go. We're trying to get a head start on today's activities."

Benji perked up like an eager puppy.

"I love you, Carolina," my mother said, her tone uncharacteristically soft. "Please take care of yourself."

"I will. Call you later."

Benji flung aside the pad of stationary he'd been doodling on as soon as I hung up. "Are we—?"

"Fifteen minutes," I ordered.

. . .

At exactly seven o'clock, Benji dragged me and Ophelia out of bed, forced us to get dressed, and pushed us out of the room and into the elevator. Ophelia rested her forehead on the glass and closed her eyes as the lift stopped at almost every floor to let more people on. When we finally arrived at the lobby, Benji pushed his way to the front.

"Sorry," I said to the other guests who fell prey to Benji's bony elbows. "It's our first day. He's really excited."

I held Benji in place as we waited for Ophelia to amble out. She left the elevator dead last, dragging her feet. I herded them to the breakfast cafeteria, where the food was less delicious but the price was included with our stay.

Everyone else had the same idea to get up early. The buffet lines extended a good twenty feet past the counters. I picked up a tray and shuffled into position.

"I'm starving," Ophelia moaned as we crept forward. "Can't we go to the Breakfast Nook so we don't have to wait in line? That's what we do every year."

"You have to pay for the Breakfast Nook," I reminded her. "This is free."

She wrinkled her nose at the pre-toasted bagels

and hot plates of scrambled eggs. "This food looks like ass."

I lightly smacked her shoulder. "Don't swear."

"My mother's abusing me," she said loudly.

A few faces turned to look at us with judgmental expressions.

"She's kidding," I said, forcing a grin. I shoved Ophelia forward and muttered in her ear, "Don't make me lock you up in the room."

We got through the line and picked a table by the window to eat our lukewarm pancakes and bacon. As I watched people line up for the chair lift, I spotted Pilar and Amos coming out of the Breakfast Nook with Marin and Nessa. All four wore matching buffalo plaid jackets and black pants.

Amos tweaked Nessa's ear then looked away, feigning ignorance, when she swung around to determine the culprit. Though I couldn't hear Pilar's answering laugh, I assumed it sounded like angels singing. From the googly-eyed grin Amos gave her, I wasn't far off. As the foursome headed toward the slopes, my heart sank into my stomach.

"Hello?" Ophelia waved her hand in front of my face. "Earth to Mom! Are you listening?"

"What? Yes. Did you say something?"

"Ugh, never mind."

. . .

AFTER RENTING three snowboards of appropriate sizes for each of us, I came out of the rental shop to find that my children had scattered in opposite directions. Benji stared into the trees, no doubt looking for birds to draw later, and Ophelia had joined a group of teenagers near the beer hall. When she saw me emerge, she ran over and grabbed the medium-sized board.

"Thanks, Mom!" she called, taking off.

"Whoa, where do you think you're going?"

She hit the brakes and jabbed her thumb over her shoulder at her new friends. "Those guys say they know some secret trails here. We're gonna check it out."

I eyeballed the teenaged boys. They looked like trouble. "Do you know those kids?"

"I do now," Ophelia said. "Chill out, Mom. Can't I make friends?"

"This vacation is supposed to be for us to hang out as a family." I hauled my board up under my arm as Benji's slipped from my grasp. "I was hoping we could board the bunny slope together."

"The bunny slope? That's for kids."

"Benji's not very good."

"So? That's his problem."

I fixed her with my Mom stare. "O, this means a lot to me."

"Hey, Greek girl!" one of the boys shouted. "Are you coming or not?"

Ophelia shot me an apologetic look as she ran off. "I'll board with you later, Mom. I promise!"

I sighed as she disappeared with the crowd of boys. Hopefully, none of them got the wrong idea about her. I tapped Benji on the shoulder.

"Looks like it's just you and me." I handed him the smallest board. "Ready to go?"

He beamed. "Let's do it."

I strapped Benji's boots into his bindings then did my own. We rode the conveyor belt lift up the bunny slope, which was easier to get on and off than the chair lift. Benji whooped as he cruised down the hill, carving uneven lines through the snow. I grinned and followed closely behind to keep other people and kids from rushing him.

The wind rushed by, stinging my cheeks and lips. I cut a few sharp turns and took pleasure in the waves of snow the board kicked up. In a few minutes, the ride was over, and we coasted to a stop at the bottom of the hill.

"Whew!" I pushed my goggles up and wiped my forehead. "That was fun. Wanna go again, Benji?"

Benji panted and unbuckled one of his boots. "I'm tired."

I tried not to let my disappointment show. "Already?"

"I think I'm gonna draw some birds. Is that okay?"

I helped him take off the cumbersome board. "That's fine, buddy. Do you mind working by the kids taking lessons? I'm going to try another hill, and I don't want you to be alone."

Benji bounded over to the group of children wobbling on their skies. I ensured one of the instructors could keep an eye on Benji then rode the chair lift to one of the tougher trails.

At the top, I gazed across North Carolina's beautiful landscape. The endless blue sky and white-capped mountains almost made me forget about the complications with Amos. I took a deep breath and hopped into place. The board slipped beneath me, so I bent my knees, set my weight low, and let instinct take over. I rushed down the trail, savoring the peace of mind the adrenaline brought to me.

AT THE BOTTOM, I considered trying one of the harder trails for a challenge but chickened out. Sometimes, they brought people off the mountain's difficult areas on a stretcher. Besides, wind burn decorated my cheeks. I needed a warm spot to relax and enjoy a pick-me-up.

Benji was right where I'd left him. The ski instructor gave me a little wave to let me know everything was okay. Benji, oblivious I'd returned, continued sketching on his stationary pad.

"Hey, buddy," I said, rubbing his head. "Do you want something to eat?"

"No."

"How are you feeling?"

His hand shook as he etched a shadow along the wing of the bird he drew. "Fine."

"I think you should eat something. Come on, let's get you a snack."

He blew an annoyed sigh, tucked away his drawing, and got to his feet. Together, we went to the eatery closest to the slopes. The cafeteria-style restaurant made it easy for everyone to eat what they wanted. I got a slice of pot roast from the meat counter, and Benji ordered a grilled cheese and tomato soup from the sandwich line. With our trays in hand, we chose a seat by the big windows that looked out on the mountain.

Benji wolfed his sandwich, dipping each bite in the soup until it was gone. He wiped his hands and hopped to his feet. "Can I finish my drawing now?"

"I suppose," I said. "But stay in view."

He pranced outside, unaffected by the cold air, and sat on a picnic table within my eyesight. In the window's reflection, I caught sight of a man at the table behind me. Surreptitiously, I looked him over. He was tall and clean-shaven, with a sharp jawline and well-kept blonde hair. When his hazel eyes connected with mine in the window, he smiled. Warmth rushed through me, and a blush rose along my cheeks.

The man stood and came over, hovering far enough away to stay polite. He gestured to Benji with a full glass of beer. "Is he yours?"

"Yup," I said, nodding. I pointed at Ophelia, who was busy trying tricks off the ramps and rails. "That gremlin belongs to me too."

"You're lucky," the man said, smiling sadly. "My wife has my son for the holidays. I won't see him until next year."

"Sorry to hear that."

"Divorced life, you know?"

I chuckled humorlessly. "Oh, I know. We're here with my ex-husband, his new wife, and her two daughters."

"Wow, that's rough." He offered his hand. "I'm Michael, by the way."

"Carolina," I replied. "How long have you been divorced?"

He pulled a chair over from another table and sat. "Ten long years, but she drives me crazy anyway, especially if our kid is involved. What about you?"

"We ended it four years ago."

"Your ex moved on pretty quickly then?"

"He was married again a year later," I answered wryly. "Guess why he left me?"

"You didn't shine his shoes."

I laughed. "He didn't want to take care of the kids while I worked."

Michael lifted one beautifully thick brow. "Wait, didn't you say he has two stepdaughters?"

"I sure did."

He set his untouched beer in front of me. "You need this more than I do."

I lifted the glass in thanks and took a long swig. As I wiped the foam from my lip, I noticed Pilar come into the cafeteria. "Speak of the devil."

Michael swung around to get a better look. "That's her?"

"Yes, sir."

He whistled. "Stiff competition."

"I'm not competing."

"I say the same thing when I'm around my ex's new boyfriend."

Though I tried not make eye contact, Pilar spotted me, waved, and made a beeline through the tables and chairs toward me.

"Uh-oh," Michael said. "I hope you've got your phasers set to stun."

I elbowed him in the ribs, forgetting that we'd only met a few minutes ago. He hid a laugh as he stood to give Pilar his chair.

"Don't let me interrupt!" she pleaded.

"I was heading out anyway," Michael replied. He nodded to me. "Carolina, it was lovely to meet you. I hope our paths cross again. Have a wonderful day, ladies."

Pilar took Michael's chair, and my stomach sank as I watched him walk away. Pilar brushed her voluminous hair over one shoulder and sighed happily. The cold tinged her cheeks pink like a delicate brushing of blush. Mine, no doubt, looked as if someone had slapped me.

"He looks happy," she said of Benji, who had flipped to a fresh page to draw another type of bird.

"This is his favorite place."

"Hm." Pilar turned toward me. "I didn't mean to accost you, but I thought it would be good for the two of us to talk alone."

My shoulders tensed. "About?"

"We both know this vacation is weird," she said, exasperated. "When Amos first said he wanted to go skiing with his ex-wife, I wasn't sure how to take it."

"It's for the kids," I said, like a broken record.

"It should also be for us," Pilar insisted. "We all work hard. I want you to enjoy yourself too. Can we pretend this is a normal thing for people to do? We're one family."

"We are?"

She placed a hand lightly on my arm. "Of course.

Benji and Ophelia mean the world to Amos. I want him to be in their lives."

"Did he say that? About the kids?"

"Not in so many words," Pilar replied, removing her hand. "But I see the effort he makes with Nessa and Marin. He's been so helpful. When I have to work late, he comes home early to make sure they're taken care of."

I shredded a napkin to pieces in my lap. For Pilar, Amos would cede his time for the kids. For me, not so much. "That's nice," I said through clenched teeth.

Before Pilar could gush anymore about my ex-husband's loyalty to his new family, Ophelia appeared at the table. Blood ran down her chin and neck.

"Oh my God!" Pilar gasped.

"What did you do?" I asked flatly, handing her a napkin I hadn't ripped to shreds.

"Busted my lip on a rail," Ophelia replied with a hint of pride as she pressed the padding to her mouth. "It was awesome. The guys got so grossed out. I think I need stitches though. It won't stop bleeding."

I looked beneath the napkin. A nasty gash decorated Ophelia's bottom lip, extending toward her chin. The mangled skin oozed fresh pulses of blood.

"Gross." I piloted Ophelia away. "Let's get you to first aid. Pilar, we'll see you at dinner tonight?"

"See you then!" Pilar called after us. "Good luck!"

Wolf Park had its own little village in the valley between the mountains, complete with locally owned shops and restaurants. The line for Emiliano's—our favorite place to eat—extended out the door, but Amos confidently strolled inside, gave his name, and got our party of seven seated within five minutes. Those waiting glared as the hostess led us to a reserved table.

"Pays to make reservations," Amos boasted. He pulled a chair out for Pilar, and she thanked him with a kiss. He did the same for Nessa and Marin. When he got to me, I shook my head.

"I'm good," Ophelia said, when Amos tried to help her into her seat.

"What happened to your face?" he asked, eyeballing the five stitches keeping her skin together.

"Accident of fate," she replied. Then she put in her headphones, propped up her menu, and disappeared behind it.

Amos looked at me for an answer.

"She fell doing a snowboarding trick," I told him. "Hit her face on the rail."

"Did you have her checked for a concussion?"

"The doctor said it wasn't necessary."

"She hit her face."

"I know, but—"

Pilar cleared her throat and picked up the specials list. "What's everyone's favorite dish here? I might try the eggplant parmesan. Should we order a bottle of wine for the table?"

Amos dropped the subject of Ophelia to peruse the wine choices with Pilar. He played tic tac toe, using crayons on the paper table cloth, with Nessa. He laughed at a story Marin recounted of him falling on the slopes. All the while, he kept one arm wrapped comfortably around Pilar's chair, gently massaging her neck.

On our end of the table, Ophelia played on her phone and Benji doodled on a napkin. The food came and went. I ate in relative silence, bearing witness to Amos's unfamiliar family dynamic.

"Look, Dad," Benji said at last, appearing beside Amos's chair as we ate dessert. "Check out what I drew."

Amos glanced briefly at the napkin. "That's nice, kiddo."

As Amos returned his attention to Pilar, Benji hung his head and trudged back to his seat. I craned my neck to see the portrait of Amos he'd drawn.

"Wow, buddy," I said. "That's impressive!"

"Whatever," Benji muttered.

Nessa, unaware of the exchange, set her fork

aside and reached toward Benji. She wiped her hands, covered in chocolate frosting, on Benji's drawings. His jaw unhinged.

I rushed toward him, prepared for what came next, but he beat me to it. Benji released an earsplitting dinosaur scream. The entire restaurant stared at us as I clapped my hand over Benji's mouth and hauled him outside.

Once we hit the cold air, he calmed. I sat him on the brick wall that bordered the restaurant and squatted to his level.

"That was an accident," I told him, brushing hair from his face. "Nessa didn't mean to wipe her hands on your drawing."

"He didn't even care," Benji murmured.

"Who, your dad?"

He nodded, tearing up.

I sighed and cupped Benji's cheek. "I know this is hard for you, but Dad is trying his best. Give him a chance to catch up with you, okay?"

Amos came out of the restaurant, brows scrunched.

"He's okay," I assured him.

"Yeah, of course he's okay," Amos said angrily. He glared at Benji, who shrank beneath his gaze. "What the hell was that? Screaming in the middle of a restaurant? That kind of behavior is unacceptable, young man."

Benji's lip wobbled as I stepped between him and his father.

"He was upset," I said. "Don't yell at him."

"You're right. I should be yelling at you." Amos prodded me in the chest. "This is what happens when I'm not around, huh? Benji can't control his temper and Ophelia almost gets a concussion? It's times like these I wonder why the judge awarded you full custody of our children. I should have fought—"

"But you didn't!" I curled my hands into fists. "You didn't fight for your children, Amos. You let all of us go like we didn't mean anything to you, so guess what? You don't get to discipline Ophelia or Benji anymore, and you don't get to judge me for how I decide to raise them."

Pilar emerged from the restaurant with Nessa and Marin beside her. Ophelia brought up the rear. All three younger girls stared wide-eyed as Amos and I yelled at each other.

"They shouldn't be acting like this," Amos spat. "You need to get them under control."

"You need to act like their father," I shot back. "But you're too busy with your new daughters to realize that. Pilar, girls, I'm sorry you had to hear that. Ophelia, let's go."

Ophelia wormed past Pilar and took my hand. Benji sniffled and latched himself onto my other arm. Together, the three of us walked to the resort shuttle by ourselves. The wind carried Pilar's voice to my ears.

"Oh, honey," she said to Amos. "You have a lot of work to do."

3

*I*n a miraculous moment the following morning, Ophelia woke before the rest of us. She flung the curtains wide, rolled onto our bed, and squatted over Benji's sleeping body.

"Hello!" she sang loudly, yanking the pillow from beneath Benji's head. "Wake up, little brother! It's your special day."

Benji tried pulling the covers over his eyes, but Ophelia's weight kept him from doing so. "I hate you."

Ophelia grinned ferociously. "You won't hate me when you see what I got you for your birthday." She drew a box, poorly wrapped in travel brochures from the resort's lobby, from behind her back and dumped it in Benji's lap. "Open it!"

Benji propped himself on his elbows and scrutinized the package. "Is it full of worms like last year?"

"No."

"Dead spiders, like the year before?"

She rolled her eyes. "It's nothing gross, I promise. By the way, it took me months to get enough spiders to fill up that box. You should have been way more impressed by my dedication."

"Don't remind me about the spiders," I ordered sleepily. When Benji had opened that "present," he'd thrown the box high in the air, scattering said spiders across my living room. For months, we vacuumed their curled bodies from hidden corners. "Ophelia, that better be something nice for your brother."

She held up two fingers in the scout's honor. "I said it's nothing gross! Come on, Benji. Just open it."

Daintily, Benji ripped the tape and unwrapped the brochures to reveal a brand-new digital camera. His eyes brightened as he lifted it out of the box. "This is for me?"

"Yup," Ophelia said proudly. "So you can take pictures of stuff and draw it later. What do you think?"

Open-mouthed, Benji gazed from the camera to Ophelia and back again. Then he threw his arms around Ophelia's neck. "Thank you, thank you, thank you!"

She awkwardly patted his back before withdrawing from his grasp. "Don't get all sentimental on me."

"I'm not!" Finished thanking his sister, Benji busied himself with the new camera and the accessories that came with it. "This is awesome!"

I pulled Ophelia aside. "Where did you get the money for that?"

She shrugged. "I've been saving up my allowance and Christmas money from Grandma. Figured Benji deserved something nice considering Dad's being a giant douchebag."

I chose to ignore the latter comment. "You saved up? For how long?"

"Long enough."

I watched as Benji happily snapped pictures through the window. "I'm proud of you, O. You're growing up."

She flicked my ear. "Thanks, Mom."

"My gifts aren't going to measure up to your sister's," I told Benji as I crawled out of bed, "but I did get you some things I hope you enjoy."

Benji let the camera hang from a strap around his neck to unwrap the presents I'd hidden in my suitcase. "Whoa, are these professional colored pencils?"

"Oil-based, like you asked for," I confirmed. "That's the brand you wanted, right?"

He ran his fingers lovingly over the set. "Yes.

Wow, it comes with a kneadable eraser and paper wipers too!"

I set another package in front of him. "One more thing."

He pulled the wrapping paper off. "A new sketchbook!"

"The pages are thicker, since you kept tearing the ones from school," I said. "This way, you won't have to draw on stationary pads anymore."

Benji hugged me tightly. "Thanks, Mom! I love them."

"Sure, buddy." I nuzzled his head. "I want us all to spend time together today. Ophelia, your friends will have to wait to hang out with you."

Ophelia lifted her shoulders. "Whatever. Davey's being a weirdo anyway. He got mad that I tried the rail before him, and he was the only one who didn't ask me if I was okay after I busted my lip open."

"You'll show him what he's missing later," I assured her.

She wrinkled her nose. "Ew. I don't care what he thinks. Are we going?"

Day Two of a ski vacation always reminded me of body parts I'd forgotten to use in a while. I flinched and twitched with every step, sore from my mid-back to my ankles. Ophelia bounced back no problem—she was ready for another day on the slopes, stitches or not—and Benji hadn't boarded long enough to feel the aftereffects.

I sniffled through breakfast and downed a Vitamin C drink as the kids loaded up on pancakes and waffles. My skin hadn't recovered from yesterday, so I applied a thick layer of petroleum jelly to my cheeks and lips to prevent further wind burn.

"Come here, Benji," I said, smothering the goo onto his face as well. "Did you put sunscreen on too?"

He stiffened, though not in response to my question. Amos, Pilar, Nessa, and Marin had arrived at the buffet. When Amos met my eyes, Pilar elbowed him and gently guided him toward us.

"Good morning," Amos said stiffly. "How's everyone doing today?"

"Super," Ophelia replied.

Amos cleared his throat. "I wanted to apologize for the way dinner ended last night. I should have handled things better. I'm sorry."

Pilar, the puppet master, looked at me expectantly. She wanted me to rise to this occasion, rather than take the opportunity to put Amos down again.

"We accept your apology," I said diplomatically.

"Would you like to join us for breakfast?" Pilar asked. "We're heading to the Nook."

I gestured to the kids' half-eaten plates. "We're fine here, but thank you."

Amos, relieved he'd gotten over the hardest part of today's challenge, patted Benji's head. "I've got a surprise planned later, so make sure you're free."

Benji brightened under his father's touch. "We're free."

"We'll see you tonight then," Pilar said, smiling as she tugged Amos and her girls away for another family day on the slopes.

Ophelia leaned toward me and muttered, "He forgot Benji's birthday again."

"No, he didn't," Benji protested, overhearing her. "He just told us he has something planned."

"Yeah, probably for his new family," Ophelia replied. "He didn't wish you a happy birthday or give you a gift. He totally forgot."

"Ophelia, can it," I hissed.

She hugged her brother tightly to her side and kissed his forehead with a wet smack. "Don't worry, Benjamin. Today is your day. All you have to do is have fun, take pictures, and draw your little heart out."

I MADE it down the bunny slope twice before my legs gave out. With shaking quads, I waddled to the cafe and bought the kids a round of hot chocolate. Benji brought out his new sketchpad and a pencil. He'd found a place to hide them in his jacket while we boarded. Ophelia glared at the group of boys on the rails and ramps. When a particularly shaggy one glanced at her, she raised her middle finger in the air.

I smacked her hand down. "Don't do that."

"Why not? He's an ass."

"You sound like a forty-year-old divorcee."

"So I sound like you?"

"I'm not forty!" I protested.

She smirked. "It's only one year away, Mom. You might as well embrace it."

I balled a napkin and threw it at her. "Can it, kid. Benji, what did you draw?"

Benji turned his new sketchpad for us to see. "It's a peregrine falcon. They're my new favorite."

"What do you know about them?"

He added a few more details around the falcon's eyes. "It's the fastest bird in the world, and the fastest member of the animal kingdom because it can dive at up to two hundred miles per hour. The females are bigger than males—"

Ophelia yawned. "I'm bored."

Benji whacked her with the sketchpad.

"Mom!"

"She started it!"

"Hey!" I shoved myself between them to prevent

the bickering match from turning physical. "Remember this morning when you were so thankful to have each other for a sibling?"

Benji harrumphed and crossed his arms. Ophelia rolled her eyes.

I checked my watch. "It's almost time for the guided hike. Finish up your drinks."

Benji chugged the rest of his hot chocolate and chewed the soggy marshmallows. Ophelia wilted in her chair.

"A guided hike?" she said. "That sounds awful!"

"It's only an hour."

"*Only?*"

She groaned and practically slid onto the floor. I kicked the bottom of her boots as Benji zipped up his coat and put on his hat.

"It'll be over before you know it," I assured Ophelia. "Come on, it's your brother's birthday."

She glanced at Benji, who extended his lower lip and let it wobble just enough to get on Ophelia's nerves. "Don't give me that look. I'm in, but if it's boring, I'm bailing."

I clapped her on the shoulder. "Everything's boring to you these days."

FIVE OTHER PEOPLE joined us at the small hut that marked the start of the trails. The guided hike wasn't particularly popular in the winter months. During the summertime, you could see all sorts of animals along the trails, but they were harder to spot in the snow. Nevertheless, Benji hopped along like an excited bunny rabbit, chattering nonstop.

"I hope we see some foxes," he said as we waited for the guide to get everyone checked in. "They're my favorite animal, other than birds. But a lot of the birds will have left the mountains during the cold months. We probably won't see a lot."

Ophelia yanked Benji's beanie over his eyes. "You won't see any like that."

He shoved the hat back. "Don't, O!"

The tour guide, a girl who looked a few years older than Ophelia, approached us. "Hi, wilderness explorers!" she said cheerfully, her cheeks pink from the chill. "I'm Bethany, and I'll be your guide on the trails today. Would the explorers like to introduce themselves?"

Benji puffed out his chest. "I'm Benji, and it's my birthday!"

Bethany gasped. "Your birthday? That means you get a special wilderness explorer badge!" From a fanny pack, she drew a cheap metal pin with the Wolf Park logo printed on it. She pinned it to Benji's jacket and saluted him. "Explorer Benji, are you ready to hit the trails?"

He saluted back. "I'm ready!"

Bethany faced Ophelia. "What about you, explorer? What's your name?"

Ophelia glared at the older girl. "Ponce de Leon."

Bethany didn't skip a beat. "You're a little far north, my friend. The fountain of youth is in Florida!"

"Thanks for the tip," Ophelia said, turning on her heel. "I'll be on my way there then."

I seized Ophelia by the hood of her coat and made her stand beside me. "This is Explorer Ophelia, and I'm Captain Carolina. We're excited to assist your crew today."

Bethany beamed at my half-assed participation and marked our names on her clipboard. "Excellent! Everyone, ready? Let's head up!"

BENJI TRAVERSED the mountain trails in awe, staring wide-eyed in every direction. When a bush rustled or a twig snapped, he swung around to face the source and brought his camera up to chest height, ready to snap a picture of some rare animal. As expected, the snowy woods revealed no secrets, and the rest of us enjoyed the glimpses of mountain scenery through the trees. Even Ophelia, who dragged her feet to let me know she wasn't having a good time, craned her neck to see the sun glisten against the snowy mountain tops.

"We do have bears here," Bethany announced, out of breath, halfway through the tour. She gestured vaguely toward our left. "This part of Wolf Park is protected land, dedicated to wildlife preservation. Don't worry about running into a bear on the slopes though! We have measures in place to keep everyone safe."

"Wish I could get mauled by a bear right now," Ophelia muttered darkly.

"Me too," Benji replied.

Ophelia elbowed her brother hard enough to knock him off the path. He tumbled into the deep snow and rolled down the hill, right into bear territory.

"Benji!"

The guided tour came to a halt as I plunged into the snow, lifting my feet high to clear the banks. Benji popped his head out and reached for my hand. I hauled him upward and half-carried him back to the path, panting with effort.

"Sorry!" Ophelia said, hugging Benji close. "I didn't mean to, I swear—"

"That's enough," I snapped. "You can go now."

Ophelia's lower lip trembled. "W-what?"

"You didn't want to come on the hike anyway," I said. "Well, you got what you wanted. You're excused. Go back to the resort. Hang out with your friends. Whatever. Let Benji finish having fun in peace."

Her brows scrunched together and her mouth hung open, like she was thinking of something to say, but my angered expression stopped her from saying it. Without another word, she turned and headed down the hill.

"Come on, buddy," I said, pulling Benji tightly to my side. "Let's see if we can spot a fox."

AFTER TWO FOX SIGHTINGS, Bethany led the tour back to the resort. For Benji's birthday, I splurged on lunch. We got a table for two at the Lift, the fancy restaurant near the top of the ski routes that you could only reach by riding the chair lift. Inside, a fire burned in a fancy hearth. Dark wood and leather interiors made the place look like an old-fashioned cigar lounge. Benji, feeling the vibes, squared his shoulders to appear older and more manly as we slid into our booth.

"We used to come here all the time," I told Benji.

"We?"

Internally, I kicked myself. "Uh, me and your dad. Before you kids were born."

Benji looked around, observing the Lift with a new perspective. "This doesn't seem like the sort of place Dad would like."

"Your dad used to be different." I picked up the menu and pretended to be absorbed in the myriad of choices. "Ooh, check it out. They have gourmet mac and cheese. You should try it."

Benji fiddled with a cloth napkin. "How is Dad different?"

I sighed. Of course it wouldn't be so easy. "People change as they get older, Benji. Your dad and I met in college. We were both a lot more free-spirited. We both had goals and dreams of our own. We put some of those things aside to get married and have kids, and your dad resented that he didn't get to pursue the career he wanted."

"He resented you?"

"No. Well, actually—" I shook my head and went back to the menu. "It doesn't matter. What matters is your dad loves you. Okay?"

Benji stared through the window. "He loves Nessa and Marin more."

"Don't say that."

"Why not? It's true. Look."

He pointed outside. The chair lift chugged up the hill, carrying Amos and Pilar with Nessa and Marin between them. As we watched, the lift deposited the happy family at the top of the slope. Amos helped Nessa clumsily slide off. She clutched him around the waist. Together, the foursome approached the easy route down the hill.

Amos tapped a stranger on the shoulder and gestured with his phone. He, his new wife, and the girls stood together and grinned brightly as the stranger snapped a photo. Amos patted the stranger in thanks. The family lined up and started down the slope.

Amos, the expert skier, could have flown past the girls and his wife as they shuffled along, but he brought up the rear instead, carving long curves to keep others away from his tribe. When we first brought Ophelia here, he had not been so patient. He'd left us in the dust, bored of skiing at a child's pace. Selfish hurt wrapped its fingers around my heart and squeezed.

I brought my fingers to Benji's chin and made him look at me. "He loves you as much as he loves Marin and Nessa, understand?"

He avoided my eyes. "I guess so."

When he looked outside again, Amos was far enough away to no longer hold Benji's attention. Our server appeared, looking harried.

"Oh, good," I said. "I think we're ready to order."

"Actually, ma'am," said the server. "There's a complication. My manager's coming over."

The manager was a man in his fifties who wore a bowtie tightly enough to keep all his blood circulating solely in his face. His rotund visage grimaced as he approached us. Not a good sign.

"Are you Miss Carolina Caccia?" he asked.

"Yes, I am."

"I'm so sorry to interrupt your lunch before it's started," he replied, "but I've just been informed of an incident in the main resort. Apparently, your daughter has been caught stealing from the ski shop. She's with security."

I ARRIVED, fuming, at the security office fifteen minutes later. When I knocked on the door, a burly woman with a buzz cut answered. Behind her sat Ophelia, who shrank to the size of a mouse when she saw the rage radiating off of me like smoke from a wildfire.

"I'm here for *her*," I snarled, pointing past the security woman.

"Come on in," the woman said. "Let's talk."

Though I wish he didn't have to be a part of this, I had no choice but to bring Benji in with me. He lingered by the door, scuffing his feet, while I rounded on Ophelia.

"What on earth were you thinking?" I shouted at her. "Stealing? What could you possibly need that I couldn't get for you? What did you take?"

Ophelia cowered in her chair.

"A pair of gloves," the security woman said. "I'm

Bo, by the way. Ophelia and I have gotten quite acquainted in the last twenty minutes."

"I'm so sorry," I said to Bo. "This isn't like her. I'll reimburse the resort for the gloves. She's only thirteen. I'm sure we don't need to get the police involved, right?"

Bo chewed on the inside of her cheek like it was a wad of tobacco. "Were this just about a pair of gloves, I'd agree with you."

"What do you mean?"

"I took the liberty of checking out some footage of your daughter around the resort," Bo explained. She turned her computer around to show me a paused security video of another store. "This is what I found."

She clicked play. Ophelia appeared in the bottom right hand of the screen, wearing her thickest snow jacket. She glanced up and stared right into the camera. She knew it was there. She looked away.

For a minute or so, she perused the store, picking up a knick knack here or a postcard there. Then she wandered over to a display of digital cameras. She checked to make sure the employees were busy with other customers, then she placed her body between the display and the security camera. A moment later, she turned around and walked out of the store.

"I don't get it," I said, stumped. "What's this?"

Bo rewound the video. "This was late last night,

shortly before the store closed. Our employees do inventory every night, and they discovered a digital camera was missing from that display. A digital camera like the one around your son's neck."

I swiveled to face Benji, who clutched his precious birthday present close to his chest. My mouth dropped open.

"You *stole* Benji's camera?" I demanded of Ophelia.

Tears leaked over her bottom lashes. "I just wanted to get him something nice for his birthday, since Dad—"

"No." I jabbed my finger at her. "You don't get to blame this on your father. *You* are responsible for your actions, Ophelia. You know it's wrong to steal."

Bo cleared her throat as Ophelia burst into tears. "Let's de-escalate here. I won't call the cops, but I need you to cover the cost of the stolen items."

"This is coming out of your allowance," I told Ophelia as I pulled out my wallet. "Bo, what do I owe the resort for the gloves and the camera?"

"Thirty-five for the gloves," Bo reported. "Seven hundred for the camera."

I dropped my wallet. "You're kidding."

"No, ma'am."

I turned to Benji. "Buddy…"

His lip wobbled as he drew the strap from around his neck and handed his brand-new camera to Bo. Then he sniffled, wiped his eyes, and let himself out of the security office.

Before Benji's birthday dinner, I seized Ophelia's arm and pulled her close. "Don't mention any of this to your father," I murmured in her ear. "He already thinks I'm doing a horrible job of raising you."

Ophelia uncharacteristically had not let out a single word since we'd left Bo. She nodded silently in agreement as we went inside. Amos, Pilar, and the girls already sat at a table for seven. This time, Amos left room for one of his own kids to sit next to him on one side. Benji's eyes lit up for the first time since he'd had to give back his own birthday present that afternoon. He climbed into the chair next to Amos and beamed up at his father.

"Hiya, sport!" Amos hugged Benji close, clearly making an effort. But did he remember Benji's birthday? "Missed you on the slopes today. Were you out there?"

"We went on a hike," Benji reported.

"Wow, did you see anything cool?"

"Two foxes," Benji said, "and Ophelia tried to feed me to the bears!"

"I did not," Ophelia added grumpily.

Amos caught my gaze and flicked his finger toward our daughter, imperceptibly asking what was wrong with her. I shook my head. Not now. Not on Benji's birthday.

"I'm glad you enjoyed your day," Amos told Benji.

Benji rubbed his hands together. "So what's my surprise?"

"You said you had a surprise planned this morning," I reminded Amos when confusion crossed his face. "For Benji's birthday."

Amos's eyes widened, and his pupils expanded. He drew his arm from Benji's shoulder. "Your birthday surprise! Right, of course."

I pressed my lips together, willing myself not to say anything. My bullshit meter read Amos's reply off the charts.

"We are going for a family sleigh ride tonight," Amos announced. "A special one for the birthday boy. Benji, you get to be the Grand Marshal."

Pilar dipped her head into her hands. Marin's eyebrows knitted together.

"I thought I was going to be the Grand Marshal," Nessa said, her voice thick.

"Uh, well—"Amos stuttered.

"You said Nessa could do it," Marin added. "I heard you."

Amos clapped Nessa on the back. "There can be two Grand Marshals."

"That's not fair," Nessa said.

Benji leaned forward. "It's okay, Nessa. You can do it. I don't want to go on the sleigh ride."

Amos seemed taken aback. "But you love horses, sport."

Benji stared at his father unemotionally. "I don't want to go. Mom, can I be excused?"

My heart sank. "Sure, honey."

Benji's chair scraped the floor as he pushed himself away from the table and left the restaurant. I rounded on Amos.

"Way to go," I snapped.

"Are you kidding?" Amos said. "How is this my fault?"

"How hard is it to remember your own son's birthday? Christ, Amos. Pull your head out of your ass."

Amos stood. "I'll go after him."

"No, you won't." I stood too, keeping Amos from leaving. "Give him time to cool off. He doesn't need your insincere apology anyway. Come on, Ophelia. I'll let you order room service."

Amos blocked our path. "Lina, come on—"

"Don't call me that," I said. "And don't act like I'm the one who keeps screwing up. Pilar told me you're great with her kids. That's amazing. I'm glad you're giving them the love they deserve. But that doesn't mean you get to pretend that Ophelia and Benji don't exist. Ladies" —I nodded to Pilar,

Marin, and Nessa— "I'm sorry, once again. None of this is your fault. I hope you enjoy your sleigh ride."

As we left, Amos said to Pilar, "Can you believe her?"

Pilar sighed heavily. "Honey, you're digging one hell of a hole."

OUTSIDE, Benji's footprints made their way up to the main resort, but he was long gone. Ophelia linked her arm through mine.

"Hey, Mom?" she said softly. "I'm really sorry about the camera. I kinda guessed Dad was gonna forget about Benji, and I wanted him to have something nice. I know it was wrong, but I didn't think I'd get caught."

I hugged Ophelia to my side. "I know you did it for the right reasons, honey. I'm sorry I yelled at you. No more stealing though, okay? I could have gotten you those gloves on sale."

"Thrilling," she said dryly.

"Is that why you did it?" I asked her. "For the thrill?"

She shrugged. "Kinda. It makes me feel good to take the big jumps and try new rails and bust my face open and steal stuff."

"Great, I'm raising a masochistic criminal."

Ophelia laughed. "It's not like that. I like the rush."

I noogied her head. "Can you find a different way to experience the rush?"

"That depends," she replied. "Can you sign the parental consent form so I can go helicopter boarding?"

"Absolutely not."

When we reached the room, Ophelia flashed her key and threw the door wide. "Oh Benji!" she sang. "Come out, come out, wherever you are! Your birthday's not over, and I still owe you eight complimentary tickle attacks, one for each year you've lived!"

Benji didn't reply. Ophelia threw back the bed covers and found nothing but pillows. Her eyebrows pulled together.

"Where is he?"

4

I checked the closet and the bathroom then ran out of places to search for Benji in the small room. For good measure, Ophelia knelt to look under the bed, but Benji couldn't have fit between the frame and the floor. She scratched her head as she stood.

"He had a room key, right?" I asked. "He didn't lose it?"

Ophelia shrugged. "Maybe.

I backtracked into the hallway and glanced toward the elevator. No sign of Benji. "He must not have come up to the room then. Where could he have gone?"

Ophelia shrugged. "He was upset. He always draws those creepy demons when he's upset."

"What creepy demons?"

She hastily doodled something on the fresh stationary pad by the phone and held it up for me to see: a jagged figure with alarmingly tall and skinny proportions, complete with blackened eyes.

"I've never seen him draw anything like that," I murmured. "Are you sure?"

"Yup. I thought they were weird trees or something, because he goes outside to draw them."

I crumpled Ophelia's doodle and tossed it in the trash, unwilling to look at it much longer. "Let's double back and check the path from the restaurant. Maybe he's still out there."

WE RETRACED our steps to the restaurant, keeping our eyes peeled for Benji. I paid special attention to the trees that lined the far edges of the resort area, but Benji's bright orange coat didn't jump out at me. We made it all the way to the restaurant, where Ophelia pressed her nose against the window.

"They're still in there," she reported. "Dad and his new family. Ugh."

"Do you see Benji?"

"Nope."

A shiver rushed down my spine that had nothing to do with the wind chill. A memory flashed through my head: a child's body, partially buried in the woods, too late to save. Bile burned in the back of my throat.

"Should we make Dad help us look—Mom?" Ophelia noticed my sour expression. "Are you okay?"

I quickly rearranged my face. "Yes. Sorry. Just worried about your brother."

"Because of what happened at your job?"

"What would you know about that?"

She drew her hood tightly around her head, obscuring most of her face. "I may have asked Grandma why you quit working for the FBI."

"When?"

"I dunno. Like a year ago?"

"What did she say?" I demanded.

"That Dad was being a jerk," Ophelia replied. "But she also mentioned you were having a hard time at work."

Another image flashed: a bloodied baby blanket.

"Did Grandma explain what I did for the FBI?"

"She said you looked for missing kids."

I wiped snow from a bench and sat. "I was good at it for a while, but when things went south at home, I got distracted. Three kids died because I couldn't find them in time."

Ophelia's eyes grew large. "What happened?"

I rubbed my temples, wishing I didn't have to recall the past. "I screwed up. I missed details I shouldn't have missed. I quit because I didn't trust myself to not mess up the next case too."

"Grandma said you quit because of Dad."

I smiled weakly. "You're too young to know these things."

She crossed her arms and fixed me with a knowing stare. "I was barely older than Benji when you and Dad broke up, but I knew something was wrong. Kids aren't stupid because they're young."

"I didn't say you were stupid."

"Then tell me why else you quit?"

I sucked on my teeth, contemplating how much to divulge. "Your dad was a big part of it. He resented me for making him take care of you all the time. I quit to save our marriage. He asked me for a divorce on the same day."

Ophelia nodded solemnly. "I remember that."

"You do?"

"Yeah, you were both crying a lot." She sat next to me and hugged her knees. "Then Benji started crying too, and you fought over who should comfort him."

"Where were you?"

"Eavesdropping from the staircase."

I draped my arm around Ophelia and drew her close. "I'm sorry for everything that's happened to our family. I'm doing the best I can for us."

"I know, Mom."

I tugged her upright. "Come on. Let's keep

looking for Benji. He's gotta be around here somewhere."

HALF AN HOUR LATER, Benji was still missing. We searched the area around the restaurant, the pathway, and the resort lobby and shops twice without luck.

"You don't think he was stupid enough to go up the hiking trails at night?" Ophelia asked. Worry made her jaw clench. The last time I'd seen her grinding her teeth like that was when Benji had been bullied by a larger boy at school. Ophelia had knocked the kid flat on his back with one punch.

I spotted Bo leaving the security office. As she locked the door behind her, I hurried over. "Excuse me, Bo?"

Bo eyeballed Ophelia, who did her best to hide behind me. "Don't tell me: you stole something else?"

"No, no," I said. "I'm sure you've seen enough of us today, but I'm worried about my son. I haven't seen him in about forty-five minutes, and we haven't been able to find him around the resort."

"Hmm. Where did you see him last?"

"At the Cove Grill," I replied. "He got upset, and he walked back to the resort himself."

"But he never made it to your room?"

"No."

Bo pulled a handheld radio off her belt and spoke into it. "Attention, security team. We've got a missing kid, goes by Benji. Four feet tall, dark hair, blue eyes. Last seen on the pathway between the main building and the Cove Grill. Fan out."

Several garbled responses came through the radio.

"10-4, boss."

"You got it."

"What was the kid wearing?"

Bo looked at me for confirmation.

"Dark jeans, a blue sweater, and an ugly orange winter jacket," I supplied.

Bo repeated the information to her team. "Don't worry, miss," she told me. "My guys are good at this. They'll comb the resort. Kids show up pretty fast, especially when it's cold out."

An hour later, I instructed Ophelia to return to the room and wait there in case Benji came back. The assignment partially mattered for this reason, but I mostly wanted Ophelia out of the lobby, where she couldn't see the worry and doubt building on Bo's face. When various security officers returned from their search, they whispered in Bo's ear and avoided eye contact with me. I knew what that meant: no sign of Benji.

In my mind, I saw the faces of every parent I'd ever had to inform of their child's death. Their expressions had been identical. They cycled through phases. Number one: shock. The blank stare, the wide eyes, the dropped jaw. Number two: denial. Shaking heads, vocal rebuttal, coming up with every excuse in the book as to why I was wrong. Number three: hysteria. Uncontrollable crying. In some cases, screaming. The screaming was the worst.

I pulled Bo aside. "Call the police."

"Ma'am, I can assure you—"

"It's been nearly two hours," I snapped. "If your team hasn't found him, it's time to get the police involved. This used to be my job. The hours directly following the child's disappearance are the most crucial. I want the police here."

Bo nodded curtly and moved off to dial the cops in private. I chewed my thumbnail, a habit I hadn't exercised since my FBI retirement. My phone rang, and I recognized the room number.

"O?" I answered quickly. "Is he there?"

"No," she said, her voice thick. "He hasn't come back. Mom, you don't think he's hurt, do you?"

"Don't say that." My hands shook. "I'm sure he's fine. Maybe he got lost. We're looking for him. Don't worry, O. We'll find him."

"Can I help?"

"Stay in the room," I instructed. "You are helping. If he comes back, call me again."

"Okay. I love you, Mom."

"I love you too, baby."

Bo returned to my side. "The police are on their way. My team has swept every inch of the resort's interior."

"What about outside? The slopes and the hiking trails?"

"You think a seven-year-old trekked into the woods wearing jeans and loafers?" Bo questioned.

"I hope he wouldn't," I said, "but what if he did? He could be lost and freezing somewhere."

"I requested the police sweep the entire ski area," Bo said. "They'll be able to take snow mobiles out there to look for him."

THE POLICE FOUND me sitting on the edge of an indoor fountain, picking quarters out of the water. When two officers approached, I dumped the handful of change.

"I wasn't stealing," I promised. "Just needed something to do."

"Keep the quarters," the older officer said. He wore his experience in the lines around his eyes and hid his stress behind a bushy mustache. "I'm Officer

Brown, and this is Officer Rivera. Can we ask you a few questions?"

"Please do."

Officer Rivera, whose round cheeks and plump lips made him no older than twenty-one, drew out a notebook and pen. "What's your son's name?"

"Benjamin Clark." I dutifully showed the officers a recent picture of Benji in his orange coat. "He goes by Benji."

Officer Rivera scribbled in his notebook. "When was the last time you saw him?"

I repeated the same answers I'd given Bo earlier.

"Could he be with other family members?" Officer Brown asked.

"He's not with his sister," I reported. "And he didn't want to be around his father."

"Why not?"

"Because he forgot Benji's birthday," I said. "That's why Benji ran off in the first place."

Officer Brown lifted an eyebrow. "So he ran away?"

"No. He wouldn't have. He's too smart for that."

River closed his notebook. "Why don't you give your husband a call? See if Benji's with him."

"My ex-husband," I corrected. "They're not together."

"You checked?"

"No, but we just came from dinner with him—"

"Two hours ago," Brown reminded me. "Plenty of time for Benji to reunite with his father. Make that call please."

With clenched teeth, I dialed Amos's number.

"Hello?"

"Have you seen Benji?" I asked, bypassing a greeting.

Amos's voice immediately hardened. "No, you gave him a get-out-of-jail-free card for dinner, remember? I haven't seen him since you all stalked off."

"Don't talk to me like that was my fault," I snapped. "I can't find our son."

"What are you talking about?"

"Benji's missing," I informed him. "We lost track of him when he left the restaurant, and we haven't seen him since. Is he with you or not?"

"I already told you he's not!" Amos's irritated breath blew static through the phone. "He's been gone for two hours? Why didn't you tell me earlier?"

"I'm handling it."

"I am his father."

"You haven't been acting like it."

Amos growled under his breath. "Goddamn it, Carolina. Put aside your snark for one minute. You should have called me as soon as you realized he was missing. Excuse me!" Jingle bells rattled. Amos was still on his sleigh ride with Pilar and the girls. "I need you to turn around. My son is missing. Carolina?" Amos added. "I'll be there in a few minutes."

"THE POLICE ARE HERE?"

Nessa and Marin, their cheeks rosy from the sleigh ride, gaped at the officers as Pilar ushered them through the lobby. Amos brought up the rear, his mouth set in a snarl.

"Come on, girls," Pilar said. "Let's get you into a hot bath." As she passed me, she mouthed *I'm sorry* and briefly patted my shoulder.

Amos was not so cordial. "Well?" he demanded. "Where could he have gone?"

"That's what we're trying to figure out, sir," Officer Brown said. "My rookie needs to take your statements, if that's all right."

"My statement?" Amos repeated. "What statement am I supposed to make when I have no idea what happened?"

"We need some information about your son, sir," Officer Rivera explained. "That's all. It'll help us find him."

Amos shook his head and rounded on me. "I can't believe this. Why weren't you keeping a better eye on him?"

"Oh, so this is my fault?" I said. "*You're* the reason he wanted to be excused from dinner."

"*You* didn't have to let him get his way so easily," Amos shot back. "You let them walk all over you. They need discipline, Carolina—"

"His father forgot his birthday!" I reminded him. "I wasn't going to punish him for feeling sad about it."

"I didn't forget. I arranged that sleigh ride—"

"Don't say it was for Benji," I spat. "I know how much Nessa likes horses. You did it for her."

Amos glared at me but said nothing. Officer Rivera waved.

"Uh, sorry to interrupt, folks," he said. "But arguing isn't going to do Benji any good. Follow me, please."

Rivera led us to a secluded corner of the lobby, where we couldn't see the rest of the police team suiting up to check the mountain. Officer Rivera made us sit next to each other on the same leather couch. Amos, usually quick to manspread, kept his knees together so as not to brush mine.

"You need to take immediate action," I informed Rivera before he could get his first question out. "Benji has Type 1 diabetes. He's insulin-dependent."

Rivera's brow wrinkled. "Does he have the means to administer insulin himself?"

"He has a pump," I reported. "But the cartridge only lasts three days."

"When was the last time you changed the cartridge?"

"Before dinner. About three hours ago."

Rivera nodded and made a note. "I'll let our guys know. In the meantime, let's get a few things straight. I understand you two are divorced?"

"Yes, sir," Amos replied instantly.

"What's your custody arrangement?"

"I have full custody," I said.

Rivera glanced at Amos. "Was that a hard decision to come to?"

Amos placed a hand on his chest. "You're asking me?"

"Yes, sir."

"Yeah, it was hard." Amos shifted, and his thigh touched mine. He jerked away. "I spent a lot of time with my kids before the divorce. I went from seeing them every day to a few weekends a year."

"Did you ask for partial custody?" Rivera questioned.

"He didn't," I answered angrily. "He told the judge that he didn't feel emotionally prepared to take care of them."

"I wasn't!" Amos insisted. "I was broken. My life was falling apart—"

"So what?" I said, volume rising. "You don't get to dump your kids because you're depressed. They're still your kids."

Officer Rivera loudly cleared his throat. "The quicker we get through these questions, the quicker you two can part ways again. Amos, do you regret not asking for more access to your children?"

"In some ways," Amos admitted. "I doubted my ability to support them when Carolina and I first separated, but I underestimated myself. I've learned so much from my wife—my new wife," he clarified. "I can handle more now."

"So you're saying you want to see your son more often?" Rivera questioned.

"Of course." Amos lifted an eyebrow. "What are you implying?"

Rivera licked his finger to turn a fresh notebook page. "Nothing, sir. Just trying to get the facts."

Amos leaned forward. "I did not kidnap my own son."

"I didn't say you did, sir."

"I can hear the accusation in your voice," Amos insisted. "The woman beside me worked missing children cases for ten years. I know the culprits are often family members, but you'd be wasting your time investigating me. I don't know where Benji is."

Rivera breathed deeply. "Sir, I have a long list of questions to get through. Maybe it's better if I talk to each of you alone."

Amos shoved himself off the couch as if he couldn't stand being so close to me for a second longer. "Sounds great to me. Come get me when you're finished with Carolina. I need to talk to my wife."

"I need you to stick around, please," Officer Rivera called after him. "Don't leave the lobby."

Amos glared over his shoulder. "I'll be in the cigar bar."

"I'm sorry," I said to Rivera. "He's touchy about our past, including the kids. For what it's worth, I don't think Benji is with him."

"We don't rule anything out, ma'am," Rivera assured me. "Am I correct in assuming you saw Benji last?"

"Yes, when he was walking out of the Cove Grill."

"Where was he headed?"

"I assumed back to our room," I replied. "I didn't give him permission to go elsewhere."

"Does he have a history of disobeying you?"

"No, that's my other kid," I joked feebly. "Benji always listens."

Officer Rivera spun the pen around his fingers. "Did Benji have a reason to run away? I heard something about a forgotten birthday."

"Benji loves his father," I said. "He adores him, but Amos hasn't paid my children much attention since he married his new wife. This trip is the first time we've spent extended time with them, but Amos hasn't taken the opportunity to reconnect with Benji or my daughter. They're just kids, but they know when they're not wanted." I cupped my neck and pressed against my pressure points. "Benji's a bit famous for his temper tantrums, but he wouldn't run away, even if he was really upset. He knows better than that."

"Like you said, he's a kid," Rivera pointed out. "Their judgement isn't the best."

"He wouldn't have run away," I said again. "I know him."

"Okay," Rivera conceded, though he didn't appear convinced. "Let's do the boring stuff. Correct spelling of Benji's full name?"

We went through the motions. I gave Rivera as many details as possible, down to the small scar on Benji's top lip from when he fell into a table corner as a toddler. Rivera took diligent notes, clarifying facts here and there. When we were through, he closed his notebook.

"Because of Benji's age and his insulin dependence, this is considered an unusual circumstance," Rivera said. "You already know that, don't you?"

"Ex-FBI, remember?"

"Right. Well, you know what it means. Finding Benji is our top priority." Rivera gazed deeply into my eyes. "I can assure you we will do whatever it takes to locate him."

I drew away from the enthusiastic rookie. "I want

to be involved. I'd like to meet with the detective when the case is assigned."

"I'm sure the force will accommodate you," Rivera said, standing. "I have to talk to your ex-husband. Will you be okay?"

I laughed humorlessly. "Sure, when you find my son."

WHEN THE POLICE returned empty-handed from their snowmobile escapades on the slopes, they requested to search our room upstairs. Officers Brown and Rivera escorted me up the elevator. Hope welled up in my chest as I flashed the room key at the door.

Ophelia had fallen asleep, fully-dressed, in the chair by the window. Her head jerked up at the heavy thump of the officers' boots. "Huh? Did you find him? Is he here?" Blearily, she noticed the cops. "Oh, great. The po-po."

"This is my daughter, Ophelia," I said. "O, these guys are helping us look for Benji. Care if they poke around?"

Ophelia spread her arms in a welcoming gesture. "Be my guest."

The officers split the room in half. It took less than a minute for them to search the nooks and crannies. Ophelia looked on in disdainful amusement.

"He's not here," Rivera reported.

"No shit," Ophelia replied.

"O," I said, a sharp, one-syllable warning.

Rivera flashed a charming smile at my daughter. "Searching the room is a mandatory part of our process, miss. We have to do it. Mind if we ask you a few questions?"

Ophelia narrowed her eyes. "Why me?"

"You know your brother best," Brown said. "Siblings are built-in best friends."

Some of the tension dissolved from Ophelia's shoulders. "I guess you're right about that. What do you want to know?"

Brown pulled up the desk chair and sat. With folded hands and a bowed head, he presented limited authoritative threat to Ophelia. "Did Benji ever talk to you about running away?"

"No." Ophelia folded her arms. "He's the golden boy. I'd be the teenage runaway."

"Did he mention he was upset about anything going on in his life?" Brown pressed. "Anything that would have made him feel unwanted or worthless?"

"Our dad's a jackass," she announced. "He basically gave us up and made Mom raise us alone. I don't know why we bothered going on vacation with him. I don't think he's asked me one question about myself."

"O, focus on Benji," I advised quietly.

"Oh, yeah," Ophelia said. "Benji was only two when Dad left, so he doesn't remember all the bad crap. He wants Dad to love him, but Dad loves his new daughters more. Benji's such a baby though. If he ran away, he wouldn't last two seconds out there."

I flinched, and Ophelia noticed.

"Sorry, Mom," she said. "I meant that he probably didn't run away. I feel like something happened to him."

"Like what?" Officer Brown said.

Ophelia shrugged. "I don't know. Maybe a mini avalanche swept him away or he got abducted by aliens. Benji loves Mom too much to run away. He wouldn't want to worry her like this."

Brown nodded. "What were Benji's favorite places to hang out at Wolf Park?"

"The kids' club," Ophelia reported. "But he never talked to the other kids. He said the clubhouse had the best view of a bald eagle nest."

"Anywhere else?" Brown asked.

"Not that I can think of."

"Okay. Now for the hard question." Brown braced himself. "Do you think Benji would have hurt himself in any way?"

Ophelia stared blankly at the officer. "Are you asking me what I think you're asking me?"

"Did Benji ever talk about—"

"Suicide?" Ophelia said incredulously. "Dude, he's seven! I mean, eight. My mom's right here. Aren't you supposed to do this more gently?"

"It's okay, O," I said, resting my hand on her shoulder. My entire chest felt ready to cave in, but I kept it together. "These are standard questions. They have to ask."

"Benji was a happy kid," Ophelia said. "The only time he's unhappy is when he doesn't have anything to draw on, or if his diabetes is messing with him, or if my dad is being a dick. He wouldn't hurt himself."

"What about—?" Rivera began.

"I think that's enough for tonight," Brown cut in, rising from his chair. He zipped his outer jacket. "We'll have patrols out all night long to look for Benji. In the meantime, sit tight. Try not to worry too much. Most missing kids show up sooner than you'd expect."

The officers excused themselves, and Ophelia scoffed.

"Try not to worry?" she said. "They clearly don't know you at all."

"Go to bed, O."

. . .

Sometime later, when the lights were out and the moon was high, Ophelia crawled off the sleeper sofa and into bed with me. I stroked her hair and stared at the ceiling, feeling everything and nothing at the same time.

"Mom," she whispered. "I'm scared."

"Me too, baby," I said. "Me too."

5

*I*n the moment between wake and sleep, there was peace. My eyelids weighed heavily, so I didn't open them. Sunlight lay across my face like a lazy cat, and I savored the warmth. Ophelia's head rested on my shoulder, one of her legs draped over both of mine. Then I remembered why Ophelia was sleeping next to me instead of Benji.

The events of last night rushed back to me. Benji's lopsided smile floated to the front of my mind, but the image shifted. His smile faded. His eyes darkened. He screamed in terror.

I dislodged myself from Ophelia, rolled over, and fumbled for the medication bottle on the bedside table. After struggling with the lid, I swallowed one of the anti-anxiety pills without water. The lump lingered in my throat.

The phone flashed red. Two messages waited to be heard. Heart thumping, I picked up the receiver and pressed the button. *Please be Benji. Please be Benji.*

"Hey, Lina." Amos's voice wavered as he used his old nickname for me. "Just wanted to know if you found Benji. I figured the cops wouldn't call me since you have full custody. Anyway, call me when you get this, please."

The phone beeped, and Officer Brown spoke next: "Hi, Carolina. This is Officer Brown with the Wolf Park Police Department. I wanted to update you on our search for your son, Benji."

My pulse pounded so loudly that I half-expected it to wake Ophelia. I held my breath.

"Unfortunately, we haven't located Benji at this time," Brown continued, and my heart sank into a pit of despair. "But we also didn't find any indication that he's in immediate danger. No sign of a struggle or blood on the premises. My guys are doing a sweep of the town, in case he headed that way. We'll keep you posted on what we find. Don't hesitate to call me if you have any questions."

The phone beeped again, and though I knew the messages had finished, I held on hope for one last-minute call to come through, with someone on the other end who had found Benji. The line was silent.

Ophelia flipped over, accidentally knocking her rock-hard shins against my knees. I grimaced as she woke up and stretched. Her fists came annoyingly close to my face.

"Watch it," I grumbled. I witnessed Ophelia's moment of realization as it crossed her face.

"They haven't found him yet, have they?" she asked.

I shook my head.

Ophelia crawled into my lap, something she hadn't done in years. Her gangly legs hung over the side of the bed. "What are we supposed to do?"

I tweaked her nose. "*You* are going to enjoy your vacation. Find your friends. Go boarding. Let me worry about Benji."

"You really think I'm gonna ditch you for those stupid boys?"

"You like those stupid boys," I reminded her. "Besides, I'll have to meet with the police again today. It's going to be boring. You might as well make the most of our vacation."

"It's your vacation too," Ophelia said.

"And it's Benji's." I patted her bony knees. "Wherever he is, he's probably scared. I need to find him as soon as possible."

She leaned her head against my shoulder. "If anyone can find him, it's you."

"I hope that's true."

The phone rang, and I lunged for it, upsetting

Ophelia's balance on my lap. She took no offense and easily rolled off me as I picked up the receiver.

"Hello?" I said promptly.

"Hi, Carolina?"

"Yes, this is she."

"This is Officer Brown with the—"

"Yes, yes, I know who you are," I said. "Did you find my son?"

"Not yet," Brown replied, and if it was possible, my heart dropped a little deeper. "You asked to meet the detective assigned to Benji's case. Her name's Petra Lee. She's the best. She wants a meeting with you."

"When?"

"Is now too soon? She's waiting in the lobby."

DETECTIVE PETRA LEE was beige from head to toe. Her blonde hair was the same shade as her pantsuit, the fabric of which was indistinguishable from her skin tone. She wore matte beige flats and carried a beige briefcase. Even her sharp, hawk-like eyes were light brown. If she stood against a sandy hill, she would disappear.

"Mrs. Carolina Caccia?" she said when she spotted me emerging from the elevator.

"Did you recognize the panic on my face?" I asked, shaking her hand.

"No, I have a copy of your driver's license," she replied drily. "I'm Detective Lee. Not Petra, not Miss Lee. *Detective*."

"Noted."

Detective Lee glanced around me and raised a thick beige brow at Ophelia. "And who is this?"

I pulled Ophelia in front of me and framed my hands on her shoulders. "This is my daughter, Ophelia. Benji's brother. They're very close."

"Do *you* know where your brother went?" Detective Lee questioned Ophelia.

"No," Ophelia replied.

"Hm." Detective Lee smirked at me. "Not so close after all, it seems."

Ophelia curled her tongue to craft an indignant reply, but I turned her toward the slopes.

"Go boarding," I ordered her. "If I hear anything about Benji, I'll come find you."

Ophelia threw a dirty look at Detective Lee then put on her gloves and headed outside. I turned to the detective, who wore an expression similar in discontent to my daughter's.

"The front desk woman was kind enough to reserve a room for us," Lee said. "Follow me."

She turned sharply on her heel and walked briskly away. I quickened my pace to keep up with her, my heavy boots thudding against the fancy marble floor as her flats made almost no noise at all.

"I'm not sure if Officer Brown told you," I began, "but I used to work missing children cases for the FBI. I'm familiar—"

"Oh, yes," she cut in. "I'm well aware of your reputation, Miss Caccia."

"Excuse me, what reputation?"

She passed behind the front desk as if she owned the entire resort and gestured for me to follow her into a small room. From the half-full coffee pot and vending machine of crappy snacks, this was an employee break room. Lee unfolded two aluminum chairs and set them on opposite sides of a card table.

"Please sit," she ordered in a tone that could not be argued with. After I obeyed, she continued. "Let's make one thing clear. I do not fold to the whims of parents, regardless of their employment background. My job is to find your son, not cater to your fragile emotions."

The brusqueness of her statement sank in slowly. I allowed her a moment of silence to reflect on her faux pas, but she appeared blank of regret or embarrassment.

"I am not your average concerned parent," I informed her. "I know the procedure for this sort of thing, perhaps better than you do. My role with the agency—"

"You are not an agent," Lee said. "We are not co-workers. You are a mother. I need you to act like a mother. It's the best chance we have of finding your son."

"I don't understand—"

"If you act like an agent during the course of this investigation, it will interfere with my work," Lee cut me off again. "I cannot have your professional opinion clouding my judgement. Is that clear?"

I sat back and crossed my arms. "Did you file this with the NCIC yet? The National—"

"I know what the National Crime Information Center is, thank you very much." She pressed her lips together and folded her arms too, mirroring my position. "And yes, we have already let them know of Benjamin's disappearance. That means the FBI is already involved with the case. That means *you* don't have to be."

"He's my son," I reminded her. "I'm involved whether you like it or not."

Finally, the sharp lines around her eyes softened slightly. "This is what I request of you, to act as his mother and not as an investigator. I need his mother. I don't need another person who thinks they know best about this case."

"I can't promise not to be both."

"I suggest you try. For Benji."

She poured coffee into a disposable cup, and I thought she might offer it to me—the worried mother—but she sipped it feverishly instead. She drank it black, an obvious cry for help. After a satisfied sigh, like an addict getting a fresh dose, she opened her briefcase and took out a laptop. She set it up so I couldn't see the screen.

"Let's get to it," she said, sitting across from me. "I got the report from my officers, but I want to go over some of these details with you personally—"

Amos barged in, fully dressed in his ski gear and his face bright-red. He pulled off his gloves and unfolded another chair. "Sorry I'm late. Did I miss anything?"

"What are you doing here?"

"Detective Lee asked to speak with me too," he replied. "Good of her to include me since you never bother to."

"Officer Brown didn't mention you," I said. "I didn't think—"

"I have as much right to be here as you do."

"Technically, you don't," I pointed out. "Since I have full custody."

Detective Lee set her foam cup in the direct center of the card table. Though her action made no sound, the movement drew mine and Amos's attention away from each other and back to her.

"That's better," she said once quiet fell. "Mr. Caccia—"

"My last name is Clarke," he said. "She went back to her maiden name after we divorced."

"Mr. Clark then," Lee went on. "I'll preface our meeting with the same thing I told your ex-wife. You are not an investigator. You are a parent. You will act as such. I cannot find your son if your hysterics get in the way. A parent's mistake can ruin everything."

Amos lifted his palms. "I completely agree. I don't intend to get in your way, Detective Lee. I want you to find my son as soon as possible. If that means you need me to distance myself, I completely understand."

Lee's gaze flickered to me. "He gets it."

"He's never worked a case like this before," I replied acerbically. "It makes sense for him to stay out of it."

"Regardless, his is the kind of attitude I respect," she said. "Moving on. Can each of you describe the last moment you saw Benji?"

Though I felt like I'd answered the question ten times over by now, I repeated the story to Detective Lee. Benji got upset at dinner, asked to be excused, and walked back to the resort.

"You let him go alone?" Lee asked.

"He got a two-minute head start," I replied. "I followed right after him."

"Two minutes was long enough for him to disappear though."

Amos ran his fingers through his thick curls. "I told you we should have gotten them cell phones.

We could have avoided all this trouble if he'd been able to call us."

"Increased screen time leads to lower levels of white matter in the brain," I told him. "I don't want our kids to be walking zombies. They don't need phones."

"They should have them in case of emergencies. Marin and Nessa have them."

I rolled my eyes. "Of course they do."

Amos's lip curled. "If Benji had had a phone, he might have been able to let us know he was in trouble."

"Bickering won't bring Benji home," Lee said before I could reply. "Neither will what-ifs. Let's get back to the subject at hand. I'll need a complete list of Benji's friends."

"Okay," Amos said. "I'll contact the kids' club and ask who he was hanging out with."

I rested my head in my hands. "He doesn't talk to anyone at the kids' club."

"He's there all the time," Amos contradicted. "He's had to have talked to some of them."

"He goes there to draw," I replied. "He doesn't have many friends, not even back home. He's a shy kid."

"That's not true." Amos snapped his fingers in recollection. "What about that funky-looking kid with the goggle glasses? Shane something?"

"Shawn," I corrected. "They haven't seen each other since preschool. His closest friend is Tommy from soccer."

"Benji doesn't play soccer," Amos said.

"He did last year," I informed him. "Before he decided he didn't like it. If you asked your kids about their lives every now and then, you might have known that."

"Are you done with guilt-tripping me yet?" he snapped.

"This Tommy," Detective Lee interjected loudly. "Does he have a last name and a phone number?"

"Gregor," I answered. "I'll get his mother's number for you, but I doubt it will shed much light on where Benji went. Tommy lives an hour away."

Lee refilled her cup. I hadn't noticed she'd already finished the first one.

"If your son was planning on running away, he might have told his best friend," she said.

"Benji wasn't planning on running away."

"You don't know that," Lee said.

"Something happened to him," I insisted. "I know my child, and I know he wouldn't run away. He got lost or someone took him—"

Amos scoffed. "Back to this, are we? I did not kidnap our son, Carolina."

"I'm not talking about you," I barked. "Can you shut up for one second?"

Detective Lee tapped the laptop keys. "Do you know of anyone else who would want to hurt Benji or had a motive for kidnapping him?"

"No," Amos said firmly.

"Not off the top of my head," I added, "but that doesn't mean he wasn't abducted. Random kidnappings do occur. I've seen it."

"From the information we've gathered so far, it seems unlikely," Lee said. She ticked off the reasons on her fingers. "He was upset about his birthday, he was mad at his father, he's prone to tantrums, and he stormed off. All signs point to runaway."

"You're wrong," I told her. "I know Benji."

Lee braced her hands against the back of her vacant chair and leaned over us. "It doesn't matter how well you know your son."

"Bullshit."

Amos looked sharply at me. "Carolina."

"No, it's bullshit," I said again. I turned to the detective. "Look, I don't know who rammed such a thick stick up your ass, but you need to find a way to pull it out. You cannot *ignore* the parents in this situation. We are your only source of true information. On some level, you need to trust that I know my son better than anyone."

She planted her forearms on the chair so her eyes were on the same level as mine. "You misheard me, Miss Caccia. I never planned on ignoring you. I'm simply doing what I see fit to find your son. Besides, I'm sure you worked with plenty of parents who were completely oblivious about their children. Who's to say you aren't just as ignorant?"

I almost slapped her. I might have if Amos hadn't pinned my hand to the table beneath his in a show of solidarity.

"Detective Lee," Amos said, dropping his smooth voice into a low, soothing register. "Antagonizing my ex-wife is not acceptable. I would appreciate you taking her views into account."

Lee nodded to Amos. "Please understand. These conditions are for Benji's benefit. I *will* find your son, no matter what it takes."

When Detective Lee finally released us from the cramped, stale coffee-scented break room an hour later, she left Wolf Park without a word of compassion, reassurance, or goodbye.

"What a strange woman," Amos murmured, gazing after her.

I whacked his shoulder. "I don't need your chivalry."

"What are you talking about?"

"Defending me to Lee," I clarified. "Don't bother. She's full of shit anyway."

"She's the one responsible for finding our son,"

he reminded me. "You should probably treat her with some semblance of respect. I'm sure she knows what she's doing."

"She's already making mistakes," I said. "*We* should be her number one resource for all things Benji. She should listen to my instincts. She should take advantage of my position with the FBI. At the very least, she should act like a human and not a robot. She called me fragile!"

Amos flushed as passing tourists glanced our way, curious about my raised voice. "You're acting fragile," he hissed. "Would it kill you to bury your pride? For Benji's sake?"

I gaped at him. "Do you care about Benji at all?"

"Of course I do!" he replied, clearly offended. "Which is why I'm doing what Detective Lee asked and staying out of it."

I pulled away from him. "By all means, Amos, enjoy your vacation. I'll be too busy looking for our son."

"Carolina!" he called after me as I walked away. "Come on, don't be like that."

"This was my job, remember?" I kept walking. "I know a lot better than you or Detective Lee think I do."

FOR THE REST of the day, I kept an eye on Ophelia

and searched Benji's favorite spots at Wolf Park, asking anyone and everyone if they had seen him. No one at the kids' club or along the hiking trails admitted to spotting his garish orange coat.

For a while, I sat near the kids' club and stared at the bald eagle's nest that Benji had been so obsessed with. The bundle of sticks was devoid of birds—it wasn't mating season—but Benji had drawn the damn thing countless times in the last few days. I half-expected him to come ambling out of the forest with his sketchbook in hand, claiming he only disappeared to get a better view.

From my vantage point, I could also watch Ophelia ride the ramps and rails with her friends. While the boys were looking at her, she grinned and taunted them, but when she thought no one was watching, her smile faded away. She gazed absentmindedly into the distance until one of her friends challenged her to try a new trick.

Between my two kids, I'd always though Ophelia would be the one to give me heart palpitations like I was feeling now. She was the wild child, the adventurer, always chasing some adrenaline rush. She acted without rational thought and made reckless decisions. I waited for the day I'd have to bail her out of jail for a petty crime or drive to the hospital because she'd gotten hurt during a stunt. I expected those things.

I didn't expect Benji to be the one to vanish without notice, the one to make me feel empty and useless as a parent. I wondered what he would look like in a coffin.

"Christ, Carolina," I muttered to myself. "Don't think like that."

I took out my phone, scrolled through my contact list, and clicked on a number I hadn't dialed in a few years. I put the phone to my ear.

"Hello?" a familiar voice answered.

"Mila?"

"Carolina Caccia," Mila said. "I thought I recognized that number. What's up? I haven't heard from you since you disappeared off the face of the earth."

I grinned at Mila's easygoing tone. No matter how hard things got, she sounded the same. "I need a favor."

"And I need a million dollars."

"My son is missing," I said, ignoring her joke.

"You're shitting me."

"I'm not," I replied. "He disappeared last night, and if we don't find him in three days, he'll run out of insulin. The detective in charge is determined to keep me at arm's length. I need your help."

Mila sighed heavily into the phone. "I'm not sure what you want me to do."

"The case has already been sent to NCIC," I told her. "You should have access to it."

"Do you want me to review it?"

"I want you to keep me updated."

She was silent for a moment. "You realize what you're asking me to do is illegal, right?"

I gazed toward the mountain, where everyone else skied happily with their families. "We were best friends, Mila," I reminded her. "Doesn't that count for anything?"

"It might," she said, "if you hadn't completely lost touch with me after you quit working for the agency. Can I still consider you a friend?"

"I needed a clean break back then," I explained. "Amos was—forget about it. It's a long story, and you know most of it already. Can you help me or not?"

"I can't promise anything," Mila said. "You know how it is here. All our information is tracked and logged."

"You don't have to send me anything," I told her. "Just call me every once in a while."

"Our calls are tracked too, C."

"Please." My voice cracked. "If the roles were reversed and Rosie went missing, I would do it for you."

Rosie was Mila's ten-year-old daughter. When the two of us worked together, we often reflected on how lucky we were to have all our children safely at home.

"I'll see what I can do," Mila said shortly.

"That's all I can ask."

After saying goodbye, I spotted Michael—the handsome man from the cafeteria who'd made me feel slightly better about Amos's new family—skiing down one of the harder routes. I watched him cut back and forth, admiring his form, until he cruised to a spot directly in front of the kids' club.

Hurriedly, I pulled up my hood and turned away, hiding my face. The last thing I wanted to do was pretend like everything was okay to placate a stranger. As I peered out of my periphery, Michael peeled off his goggles and wiped sweat from his forehead. He glanced at the kids' club, but if he recognized my bulky coat, he didn't bother to come over. Instead, he unbuckled his skis and headed back toward the chair lift.

I blew a sigh of relief. At least one thing had gone my way today.

6

The phone rang and rang, like the shrill holler of an angry seagull. It vibrated at the head of the bed, next to my pillow, until I blindly groped to find it and slid my finger across the screen to answer the incoming call.

I wiped drool from the corner of my mouth. "Hello?"

"Carolina Rosetta Caccia, where on earth is your son?"

I held the phone and my mother's strident voice farther from my ear. Ophelia, who'd slept beside me again, buried her head beneath the covers.

"I don't know," I told my mother firmly. "That's what the cops are trying to figure out."

"It didn't occur to you to call me?"

It hadn't. Embarrassment and pride flushed

through my body. Benji loved my mother. My mother loved Benji. This should have been one of the first calls I made.

"It's been crazy. I've had to—wait a second," I said, brow furrowing. "How do you know Benji's missing? Did Amos call you?"

"He would never be so bold," she replied. "No, the Wolf Park Police Department phoned me. Some woman named Petra nearly ripped my ear off. God, what an intolerable woman. You should complain and get someone else to find Benji." Without warning, she burst into tears. "Oh, Carolina. How could you let this happen?"

Once more, I held the phone a few feet away as her sobs escalated. When she calmed, I said, "Mom, I do not need you to blame me for this. I assume Benji isn't with you?"

"N-n-no," she sputtered. "How would he have gotten here?"

"He's a smart kid," I said. "He could have gotten on a bus. What about our other relatives? Do you think Benji would go to any of them? Your sister, maybe?"

"I'll call her," Mom said, sniffling as she contained herself. "What happened, Carolina? Why is he missing? Where's my grandbaby?"

I dropped my head and squeezed the bridge of my nose, willing myself to keep it together. With everyone else, it was easier to act like the hardass ex-FBI agent who worked these cases so often that I became numb to them. But my mother, as much as it pained me to admit it, possessed the parental power to see right through me.

"He disappeared, Mom," I said thickly. "One second, he was right in front of me. The next, he was gone. I don't know what happened."

"What do you *think* happened?" she asked. "This detective woman seems to be under the impression that he ran away."

I shook my head though she couldn't see. "I don't think he ran away. He knows he can't go longer than three days without switching out his insulin cartridge. I think something happened to him."

"Like what?"

"I don't know." I breathed deeply, in through my nose, out through my mouth. "He was on the path between the resort and the restaurant when he vanished. My first instinct is that somebody took him. How else would he have disappeared so quickly?"

"Who would do such a thing?" Mom cried.

"Some people are awful," I replied. "They do it because they can. They have reasons: extortion, human trafficking, illegal adoption, or worse—"

"Don't say it," she warned me. "Don't you dare tell me some sicko wants to hurt Benji."

"I wish I didn't have to entertain these ideas." I reached for my medication and unscrewed the lid. "But these are the facts. Benji is probably not safe. Can you call everyone on your side of the family to see if they've heard from him? We need to exhaust every avenue."

"I will," she promised. "What are you going to do?"

I watched Ophelia as she stretched and mumbled in her sleep. My heart swelled. In a moment, she would wake up to another day without her brother. If I lost faith, she might never see her brother again.

"I'm going to find him," I declared. "The police told me to stay out of it, but I don't care. I'm going to do whatever it takes to get my son back."

"That's what I was hoping you'd say."

I LET Ophelia sleep for as long as possible while I dialed every person in my contacts that might have seen or heard from Benji. I spoke to people I hadn't addressed in years, informing them of Benji's disappearance. When I phoned Amos's mother Cordelia, gritting my teeth in anticipation, I received a gentle surprise.

"Carolina, sweetheart," Cordelia said in her slight Southern twang. "You don't have to explain a thing. Amos called me earlier and let me know everything."

"Amos called you?"

"Yes, of course," she replied. "Benjamin is incredibly important to him. To us, as well. We want to make sure he gets home safely, so let us know if we can do anything to help. I mean it, honey. Don't you dare hesitate to call. Are you taken care of? Are you eating?"

I sniffled, taken aback by Cordelia's kindness. "We're still at Wolf Park, so some of the meals are included. It's nice not to have to cook though."

"Well, let me know if you need me to send you a care package when you get home," she said. "I'll deliver it myself. You need your strength."

"Thank you, Cordelia." I fiddled with the crack on my phone case. "I'm sorry we haven't spoken in so long. I should do a better job of getting you and the kids together."

"I understand why you pulled away," she replied softly. "But I do love to see my grandbabies. Amos doesn't need to be our go-between, Carolina. I'll be happy to spend time with you and the kids alone."

"I'll remember that," I said. "Thank you. And if Benji calls you or contacts you in any way—"

"You'll be the first to know."

"Thank you," I said again, unable to think of anything else. "Cordelia, thank you so—"

"That's enough now, sweetheart," she said firmly. "Go find Benjamin. I know you can do it."

She hung up before me, though not rudely. My hand trembled as I set the phone down.

"Who was that?" Ophelia had woken at last. Hugging a pillow to her chest, she regarded me with doleful eyes. "Has someone seen Benji?"

"Not yet," I said. "That was your other grandmother."

She wrinkled her nose. "Grandma Cordelia? I thought we weren't talking to her because she took Dad's side in the divorce."

"It seems I misconstrued things," I informed her. "She wants to be part of your life, regardless of your father's choices."

"Huh." Ophelia considered this. "I suppose she sends a lot of money on my birthday. That's always nice."

"You shouldn't rank family on how big of a check they send you on holidays."

"Why not? It's a perfectly reasonable way to judge them."

I flicked her ear. "Come on, moneybags. Let's get some breakfast."

Despite her jokes, Ophelia's energy and attitude dragged. Her shoulders slumped toward the ground. Her head remained bowed until we got into the elevator, when her eyes sharpened as she scanned the lobby below for signs of her brother. I decided to treat her with breakfast at the Nook, but she was too preoccupied with Benji's absence to enjoy her food. Each time a boy around Benji's size passed nearby, she jerked her gaze away from her pancakes to check if it was him.

"You haven't touched the chocolate chips," I said, scooting the ramekin full of candy toward her. In the past, I hadn't allowed her to order them. "Don't you want to take full advantage? This is a once-in-a-lifetime opportunity."

She didn't entertain my feeble joke, picking at her pancakes. "I'm not hungry."

"You should try to eat," I said. "You'll need your strength on the slopes."

She set aside her fork and knife. "How am I supposed to go boarding when Benji is missing?"

"You did it yesterday," I reminded her.

"Yeah, because I figured you'd want me out of your hair," she replied. "I know you, Mom. You're probably putting together a case file for Benji already. I know you're trying to put on a brave face for me, but I can't pretend everything's okay. I want to help find Benji."

I reached across the table to hold her hand. "Honey, you shouldn't have to. This is going to be our only vacation for the year. You should enjoy it."

Her eyes shimmered with tears. "Don't you get it?

I can't! Not without Benji. Yeah, he's my annoying little brother and sometimes I wish he would disappear, but I didn't mean it! I didn't actually think—" She choked up and wrenched her hand away from mine to cover her face as she lost control of her emotions.

The server stopped by with the check and gazed at Ophelia with a hesitant expression. "Everything okay? Were the pancakes not good?"

"Can we get a to-go box?" I asked. As the server happily excused herself, I slid out of my side of the booth and into Ophelia's. She buried her face in my sweater. "It's okay, O. You can cry."

I held her head as she sobbed freely. I hadn't seen her cry in years. She was my enigmatic child. Usually, I had to wrench emotions out of her. This was a new challenge.

The bell over the door jingled, and my jaw clenched when I saw Amos and his new family come in. I half-hoped they wouldn't notice us, but Amos's gaze immediately drifted toward our booth, as if some magnetic force drew his head around to face us. When he spotted Ophelia, crying as quietly as possible, a crinkle appeared between his eyebrows. I recognized that expression. He wore it when he wanted to do something but didn't know how to make a situation better.

As Pilar and the girls settled into a booth on the

other side of the Nook, Amos came over to us. He lingered awkwardly a few feet away from the table.

"Is everything okay?" he asked quietly.

"Does it look like everyone's okay?" I replied.

He knelt beside me and tugged on Ophelia's shoulder. She reluctantly pulled her tearstained face from my sweater and stared at her father with a glum expression.

"What do *you* want?" she asked viciously.

He lifted his eyebrows. "To let you know I'm here for you. What do you need, O?"

She glared at him. "I need my brother back. Can you do that?"

"I'm trying," he promised. "The police are—"

"No, Mom's trying," Ophelia interrupted. "You're not doing anything. Big surprise."

"Ophelia, I don't think—"

She jabbed his chest with her index finger. "This is *your* fault. Benji wouldn't have stormed away if you'd remembered his stupid birthday. He wouldn't have gotten taken. He would be *here* right now if you had just—" Her voice hitched as she lost control again, and she hid in my sleeve. "Go away," she mumbled to her father. "Go away. I hate you."

Amos's wide-eyed shock quickly morphed into anger as he looked up at me. "What did you say to her? Did you tell her this was my fault?"

"No, I did not."

"She didn't come to that conclusion on her own," he replied hotly.

I tucked Ophelia's head more firmly against my chest. "She is thirteen years old, Amos, and perfectly capable of forming her own opinions. I can't change how she feels."

"You're poisoning the well against me," he hissed. "That's not fair. I'm doing the best I can."

"Ophelia doesn't seem to think so," I shot back. "And I haven't poisoned anything. I keep telling the kids they need their father. I ask them over and over to give you another chance. *You* keep disappointing them. What am I supposed to do about that, huh?"

Amos's rage radiated off of him like heat waves. His face turned bright-red as he stood and stormed away. By the time he made it to Pilar and the girls, he'd rearranged his face into a smile. I wondered where he found the strength to do that.

My phone rang, and I answered despite the unknown number flashing on the screen.

"Good morning, Miss Caccia," a stern voice said. "This is Detective Lee. I'm calling to—"

"Did you find anything?" I couldn't help but ask.

"If you'd let me finish," Detective Lee grumbled. "We haven't generated any leads on your son yet. There is no indication that he has been taken from the resort area, and our patrols haven't located him in the surrounding city. I don't want you to worry—"

I chuckled cynically. "You're not a mother, are you, Detective Lee?"

She didn't entertain me with an answer. "You asked to be involved with the investigation. Well, I have two jobs for you."

"You do?"

"Yes, I need access to Benji's medical and dental records."

My heart thumped against my rib cage, and my stomach lurched. Dental records were used to identify corpses when their bodies were no longer recognizable.

"I'd also like you to print out Missing Child posters of Benji and place them around town," Detective Lee continued when I found myself unable to reply. "That'll help get the word out. I suggest you offer a reward. It will bring in a bunch of tips, most of them useless, but if anyone thinks they've seen Benji, they'll call. Put the station number. You don't want these whackos calling your personal line."

"That's it?" I asked shakily. "Get his records and put up posters?"

"You wanted to be useful, right? This is what you can do."

It was busy work, assigned to me to make me feel proactive about Benji's disappearance. I'd asked the parents of my cases to do the same thing in the past. On rare occasion, missing children posters brought in an accurate tip. Mostly, people called you with bogus information, hoping for a cash reward.

"Okay," I agreed. "I'll do it. And I'll get you his records as soon as possible."

"Thanks for not arguing," she said and hung up without a farewell.

Ophelia, eyes puffy, looked up at me. "What's going on?"

I tucked my phone into my pocket. "They want me to make posters of Benji and hang them up in town. Do you want to help?"

"I'm in."

OPHELIA TURNED out to be incredibly useful. Her knowledge of poster-making was far better than mine. Within ten minutes of fiddling with a program on my laptop, she generated a poster with a recent picture of Benji and *Missing Child* in big block letters, along with tearable strips at the bottom with the police station's phone number.

"Does it look okay?" she asked, hovering the mouse over the Print button. "Anything you want to add?"

"Put my cell number alongside the station number. Actually, put it first."

"Are you sure? I thought the detective said—"

"I don't trust Detective Lee to tell me everything," I said. "If someone sees Benji, I want to be the first to know."

Ophelia shrugged, typed my number in, and saved the document. "How does it look?"

"Perfect. Print it."

The city of Wolf Park, nestled at the base of the mountain, was dreamy and beautiful. Snow blanketed the historic downtown area, where locals and tourists blended together without effort. Storefronts boasted New Year's sales and temporary stands advertised discount fireworks. While everyone else shopped and enjoyed brunch at the various eateries, Ophelia and I papered every telephone pole, streetlight, and bulletin board with the posters of Benji. An hour later, we had only covered a portion of the main street, but the bitter wind drove us into the nearest cafe.

"I hate this," Ophelia muttered as she drew off her gloves and warmed her hands around a mug of coffee. Normally, I wouldn't allow her to drink it—she was too young to develop a Starbucks addiction—but this was a special occasion. "It feels pointless. We'll never cover the whole town with just the two of us. My nose is going to fall off."

"Chin up," I said. "It might take a while, but we can do it."

She patted the stack of posters beside her. "Think this is going to work? Will someone actually call?"

"We can only hope."

Ophelia sipped her drink. "I miss his stupid face."

"I know, baby. I do too."

She glanced through the window and spit her drink out. "Ugh, are they following us or something? It's like we can't get rid of them."

Pilar, Nessa, and Marin, sans Amos, had stepped out of a local makeup shop across the street and were headed toward the cafe. The girls carried several bags from the stores along the avenue.

"Spoiled," Ophelia muttered under her breath. "I bet Pilar buys them whatever they want."

Pilar tugged her daughters to a halt as she caught sight of Benji's poster on a lamppost. She read the details with a furrowed brow. As if she sensed us watching her, she looked right into the cafe window.

Ophelia sank lower in her seat. "Oh, shit. She saw us!"

"Would you stop being ridiculous?" I said, but as Pilar walked the girls toward the cafe, I felt myself slump over as well. I was not in the mood to parley with Pilar.

Nevertheless, Pilar beelined for our table,

bringing Nessa and Marin with her. She marched right up and said, "We would like to help."

"Sorry?"

Pilar nodded to the stacked posters besides Ophelia. "I noticed you've only covered a little bit of the town so far. If we all work together, we can cover more ground."

I exchanged a look with Ophelia, silently asking her permission.

She shrugged. "Many hands make light work."

"Amos says that," Nessa chimed in.

Ophelia slid farther into the booth and patted the empty seat for Nessa to join her. "Where do you think I got it? I wouldn't say something dumb like that."

Marin climbed in on Nessa's other side. "Does he also tell you that shoveling snow builds character?"

Ophelia rolled her eyes. "Yeah, so does doing homework, emptying the dishwasher, and raking leaves. Don't fall for that crap."

"Hey," I warned Ophelia. "Don't corrupt them."

Pilar chuckled as she sat next to me. "It's fine. They need a bit of excitement. So? Where shall we start?"

SOMETHING FUNNY HAPPENED over the course of the afternoon. As the five of us traveled the streets to disperse the posters of Benji, a connection grew. Ophelia raced Nessa and Marin to put up as many posters as they could. Their breath condensed as they laughed and playfully pushed each other out of the way. Nessa asked the older girls about middle and high school. Ophelia and Marin helpfully explained what freshman year might be like.

"Don't pay attention to the older boys," Marin advised. "They're not worth it."

"Don't pay attention to boys at all," Ophelia added. "They're kinda stupid, and they're always trying to cheat off your papers."

"Bring your lunch," Marin said. "Everyone will tease you, but it's so much better to eat Mom's leftovers than the crap they serve you in the lunch line.

"If you forget your lunch and you *have* to eat the school's, get the pre-packaged PB and J sandwiches," Ophelia supplied. "They have enough protein and carbs to get you through the rest of the day, and you won't risk dying from food poisoning."

Pilar chuckled as she stapled another poster to a telephone pole. "Remind me to thank Ophelia for her frank opinion later," she told me.

"Sorry," I said wryly. "She's a bit of a loose canon."

"Oh, I'm not worried," Pilar replied. "It's good for the girls to get a different perspective. Ophelia tells it like she sees it. It's refreshing."

Ophelia spun on her heel and walked backward. "Are you talking about us?"

"No," Pilar and I chorused.

Ophelia rolled her eyes and faced front again.

"So where's Amos today?" I asked, hoping to sound casual. "He wasn't in the mood to shop?"

"He didn't tell you? He's looking for Benji." She caught sight of my confused expression and sighed. "Ever since Benji went missing, Amos has been scouring the town whenever we don't have plans as a family. I took the girls shopping today so he could keep searching without feeling bad about leaving us."

I stared at the ground, stepping directly into Ophelia's footprints in the snow. I didn't know what to say, especially after reaming out Amos this morning. "God, I'm such an ass."

"Why?" Pilar asked, genuinely curious.

"I've been hard on Amos," I admitted. "So has Ophelia. It's not right, but we both partially blame him for what happened."

"You should," she replied.

I stopped short. "What?"

Pilar linked her arm through mine and pulled me along. "Amos is hard-headed. I told him over and over to spend time with Ophelia and Benji. He kept saying you wouldn't want to see him."

"The whole point of this vacation was so he could spend time with the kids," I said. "And so I could get to know you and *your* kids. Why else would I have proposed the idea?"

Pilar shrugged. "You know how men are. It's impossible to get anything through their thick heads. But don't be too hard on Amos. He simply doesn't understand what you want him to do."

My phone vibrated before I could reply to Pilar's request. I recognized the number on the screen.

"Hey, Mila," I said. "You got something for me?"

"Oh, I got more than something," she replied mischievously. "Are you ready for the big news?"

"Unless you found my son, I'm not sure I can handle any big news."

"You're going to like my news," she assured me.

"Well, hurry up and say it," I replied. "You know I'm not a patient person."

"So I did some digging," Mila said. "Pulled some strings with my boss, that kind of stuff. Anyway, guess who got themselves assigned to Benji's case?"

"You?" I guessed hopefully.

"Damn straight," she said. "I'll be in Wolf Park by tomorrow morning. Don't you worry, Carolina. I'm going to find Benji."

7

On the morning of the third day following Benji's disappearance, no phone call woke me, but a nightmare did. My eyes shot open as I realized that Benji would run out of insulin by the end of the day. Without it, his blood sugar would spike. If we didn't find him soon, it would almost guarantee a medical emergency.

A wave of nausea washed over me. I closed my eyes and did a breathing exercise that was supposed to calm my anxiety. Inhale for four counts, hold for seven, exhale for eight. When I held my breath, my heart pounded. I exhaled early, unable to stand the tight feeling in my chest for that long. I checked my phone, but no one had left any messages.

"Any news?"

For once, Ophelia had woken before me. The

dark circles beneath her eyes told me she'd been awake for a while. She sat in the chair by the window, hugging her knees to her chest.

"Not yet," I replied.

"No one called about the poster?"

"They haven't called me," I said. "But they might have called the police station."

She rested her chin on her knees. "We're checking out tomorrow. Are we going to leave without Benji?"

The thought sent my head whirling into a storm of possibilities. Mainly, I imagined living the rest of my life without ever knowing what happened to Benji. The idea of leaving Wolf Park without him made me sick to my stomach.

"We have all of today to look for him," I reminded Ophelia. "He needs his insulin. Maybe he'll come back."

"If he ran away, he would have already come back," she said glumly. "Can we stay until we find him?"

I wanted to say yes. "No, honey. I'm sorry, but school starts soon. You can't miss it."

"My brother being kidnapped seems like a good enough reason to skip school."

"We don't know that's what happened." I kicked the blankets off my sweaty legs. The heater had gone into overdrive overnight, a telltale sign that a fresh layer of snow had been deposited on the mountain. I prayed that Benji was somewhere safe and warm. "I don't want to leave without Benji either, but I have to get you home."

"I don't know if I can do it," she said. "I can't leave without my brother."

I stroked her hair away from her forehead. "I'm here for you, O. I got your back."

My phone buzzed. Ophelia looked up hopefully.

"It's a text message," I told her. "From Mila. Do you remember her?"

"Sure, she always gave me ice cream."

"She's working on Benji's case."

"Good," Ophelia said firmly. "I don't like that detective lady. I hope Mila sets her straight."

I glanced at the text message and frowned. "Looks like you might be in luck. Get dressed. We need to go to the lobby."

I WOULD RECOGNIZE Mila's voice anywhere, especially when it resonated through the resort's lobby with such authority and arrogance. Ophelia and I had barely stepped off the elevator when the argument reached my ears.

"I don't give a damn what Wolf Park PD's protocols are! This is a federal case now. Any information you've gathered needs to be included in the file!"

Mila stood six feet high with long dark hair and cheekbones sharp enough to cut glass. She wore high-waisted jeans, a chunky sweater, and heeled boots that no one but her would dare to traverse icy sidewalks in. She did not look like an FBI agent. Often times, she was mistaken for one famous model or another. Mila got what she wanted through charm, and when that didn't work, she bulldozed her way in.

Across from Mila, wearing an indignant look of disgust, stood Detective Petra Lee. In another beige pantsuit that might have been the same one she wore two days before, she represented the other end of female investigators. Stern and stalwart, she did things by the book to prove she was as worthy as her male counterparts.

"This happens every time the feds get involved," Detective Lee complained. "You walk all over our cases, pilfer our information, and muddy our leads. I won't have it!"

"From what I can tell, you don't have any leads," Mila shot back, planting a hand on her hip. "Three days, and you don't have a single thread to follow? Sounds like the Wolf Park PD needs to go back to the academy."

Detective Lee practically trembled with rage. "We have followed the law to a tee. We are doing everything we can to locate Benjamin. We don't need you—"

"The law obviously isn't helping you," Mila said. "You said you didn't find any evidence. Well, we have pictures from the night Benji disappeared. Did you not notice the set of footprints leading from the resort path and into the forest, right where Carolina said Benji disappeared?"

Detective Lee gaped at Mila. "We looked at those pictures from every angle. We wouldn't have missed something like that."

Mila smirked and patted Detective Lee on the shoulder. "Don't worry, Petra. We can take it from here. You can go back to your small-time cases."

"You—absolute—bimbo."

Detective Lee's hands curled into fists, as if she wanted nothing more than to punch Mila in the face. I hurried between them.

"I see you two have met," I said. "Kindly realize you are discussing my son's disappearance in public, where anyone—including his possible kidnapper—can hear you."

Mila, several inches taller than me, scooped me up and spun me around as if I weighed no more than a child. "Carolina! I was going to call you, but Petra here found me first."

"It's Detective Lee," Petra spat.

"But we're working together," Mila said seriously.

"I like to be on a first-name basis with my coworkers."

I elbowed Mila at the waist, since I couldn't easily reach her ribs. She could be a pain in the ass when she wanted to be. "Take it easy on Detective Lee. She doesn't know what you're like."

The detective looked from me to Mila. "The two of you know each other?"

"We were partners at the agency," Mila said, draping her arm around my neck. "This woman taught me everything I needed to know."

Petra crossed her arms. "The agency should assign someone else to the case. This isn't right. You're biased."

"Exactly," Mila pointed out. "I know Carolina's family already. I know Benji. I have an advantage that other investigators don't have. Sorry to disappoint, but you're stuck with me." Mila glanced behind me and saw my daughter. "Damn, is that you, Ophelia? When did you grow up?"

Ophelia grinned sheepishly and high-fived my old friend. "What's up, Mila? You still look super cool."

Mila twirled on the spot and posed for O. "Thank you, darling. I do my best. What are you up to today?"

"Can I help you?" Ophelia asked, bouncing on her toes. "I want to find Benji too."

"Absolutely not," Petra answered.

Mila knelt down to Ophelia's level. "Tell you what. I need someone to stay at the resort while I go out on patrol to look for Benji. Would you be able to do that?"

Ophelia's smile dropped. "I have to stay here?"

"Someone does," Mila replied. "This is home base. If any clues turn up, I need someone to alert me. Are you up to that challenge?"

"I guess I'll board down each route and look for him." She looked at me. "Is that okay, Mom?"

"As long as you stay within view of an employee at all times," I told her. "Promise not to wander off."

"I won't."

I kissed her forehead. "Be careful."

As Ophelia went off to get her board, I was left with Petra and Mila. Mila glanced at her wrist though she wore no watch.

"It's about that time," she said cheerfully. "Ready to ride along, Carolina?"

Petra's mouth dropped. "You're bringing her on patrol? That's not—"

"Protocol?" Mila guessed tartly. She stepped closer to Petra and lowered her voice. "Listen here, Detective Lee. Leaving Carolina out of this investigation is the worst decision you've made thus far. You do whatever you need to do to cover your ass, but I'm not afraid to take her along for the ride. Understand?"

Before Petra could reply, Mila linked her arm through mine and pulled me away. Smirking, I happily followed my old friend to the parking lot.

"Damn, it's amazing what a badge can do," I remarked as we got into her unmarked company car. "That woman's been a thorn in my side for two days straight. It'd be one thing if they had a single idea of where Benji might be—"

"But they don't?" Mila finished.

"Did you really find footprints on the security footage?"

Nodding, she fired up the ignition. "Did a lot of finagling to clear the picture up, but we got 'em. Don't get your hopes up though. Someone did their best to throw us off their trail."

"What do you mean?"

"The area was trampled with boot prints," Mila explained as she pulled out of the resort's parking lot. "Like a parade went through. Benji's footprints disappeared in the mess."

I twisted around to watch the mountain recede behind us. Leaving Ophelia to fend for herself felt like the worst idea in the world, but Wolf Park was one of the safest places for her to stay. Then again, I'd thought the same when I allowed Benji to walk away from the restaurant on his own.

"You think someone covered up Benji's prints?"

"I think it's a mighty coincidence," Mila replied. "You know how I feel about coincidences."

"They rarely exist."

"You got it." Mila turned onto the main road that circled the mountain and ran through the woods. She kept her eyes peeled, driving slower than the speed limit to make sure she didn't miss anything. "Catch me up. How's life after the FBI?"

"Honestly? It's boring." I scanned the tree line for a glimpse of Benji's orange jacket and ignored the growing feeling of emptiness in my stomach. "I teach criminology courses at a community college. It's a demotion."

Mila shook her head. "You never should have left."

"I had to."

"You didn't *have* to," she said firmly. "Your husband was being a giant baby."

I rested my head against the window and let the cool glass soothe the heat from my skin. "He had a good point. I wasn't balancing my work and home life."

"Sometimes I wonder if you should have had kids to begin with." She saw the devastation on my face and quickly added, "You're not a bad mother. I meant that the agency hasn't been the same without you. Ever since you separated from Amos, things have been headed downhill. Our stats are terrible. We take twice as long to solve cases than when you were with us. My new partner" —she tilted her chin back and let out a groan— "is a complete moron. I don't know how he passed high school, let alone a competency exam for the agency."

I half-smiled. "I'm sure he's competent. You're just impossible to work with."

She feigned offense, pressing a hand against her heart. "Moi? I am a joy. Pure sunshine. I am a walking ball of light."

"I'm pretty sure Petra almost punched you in the lobby," I reminded her. "How long did you spend with her? Ten minutes?"

"Five," she corrected. "And it's not my fault if other people can't keep up with the way I work. Missing children cases are delicate. You know that. Petra and the rest of Wolf Park PD have been slacking. If I had been involved from the get-go, we would have already found Benji."

"You know local cops," I commiserated. "They always think they know best."

"Hmm." She glanced toward me. "What's your instinct telling you?"

"About Benji?"

"Yeah, but take a step back," Mila advised. "Pretend he's not your kid. Think about it as an investigator, not as a mom. If this case was assigned to you, what would your first hunch be?"

I considered it, pulling away from Benji emotionally to examine the facts. He was young, attached to his mother and sister, and insulin dependent. He was upset when he vanished. Strange tracks covered the area where he was last seen, obscuring what might have happened to him.

"I think someone took him," I said at last. "I know people think I'm biased because I'm his mother, but he wouldn't have run away. I think someone snatched him off the trail when he was walking to the resort alone."

"Okay." Mila nodded. "Why? Who would have a motive to do such a thing?"

I shrugged, trying to remain distant as I thought about the possibilities. "Anyone who could benefit from it. Have you checked the database for—"

"Other abductions in Wolf Park?" she finished. "Yes, I have. It doesn't happen. This place is squeaky clean. The crime rate is practically non-existent. No patterns or likely suspects."

"Shit," I muttered. "No one to investigate at all?"

"Nope. Not yet, anyway."

We emerged from the thick trees, and Mila turned onto the main street. The posters of Benji from yesterday were wet with snow. The ink ran, completely ruining the photo of him and blurring the numbers below.

"That explains why I haven't gotten any calls," I muttered.

"You put those up?" Mila asked, squinting at the nearest wrecked poster. "Did you want a bunch of pranksters blabbing on your voicemail?"

"It was Petra's idea," I said. "I had to do something."

Mila reached over the center console and squeezed my knee. "You're doing great, Carolina. We'll find him."

OUR FIRST ORDER of business in town was to check the local hospital. Petra and the Wolf Park Police Department had already done so, according to the receptionist at the front desk, but Mila insisted on walking the hallways anyway. We glanced into patients' rooms, flashed Benji's photo, and asked random people if they had seen him. No one recognized my son's photo, and he didn't seem to have graced the hospital's halls in the recent past.

After we cleared the hospital, we walked the streets with Benji's picture in hand. Mila had a different idea here: instead of stopping adults to ask about Benji, she approached teenagers and younger children with their parents' permission.

"Have either of you seen this boy?" she asked a pair of twins around Benji's age as they came out of a toy shop with their mother.

The twins shook their heads. Their mother squinted at the photograph.

"He looks familiar," she said. "But I haven't seen him."

We continued on, without luck. Despite my thick socks and snow boots, my toes began to go numb. Blisters formed on my heels. Every step made me wince. Every wince made me think of Benji, alone and scared, most likely taken by someone who meant to harm him. I walked on.

Outside a soda shop, a group of teenagers loitered. I recognized a few of them as Ophelia's new snowboarding friends from the resort.

"Hey, I know you," one boy said, pointing at me. "You're Greek Girl's mom! I'm Trent. Can you ask her if she likes me?"

"You ask her," I returned. "But don't expect the answer you want. Where is Ophelia? She's not hanging out with you guys?"

The boys shook their heads, each wearing the same glum expression.

"She blew us off today," Trent said. "Is she okay? She's been weird lately."

"Her younger brother went missing." I showed

the boys the picture of Benji. "Have any of you seen him around? He's only eight years old."

The boys studied the picture with intense expressions. One of them, short and stout with long sandy hair, lit up with recognition.

"I saw him!" the boy exclaimed. "He was with a tall dude near the pharmacy."

My heart rate quickened. "Are you sure?"

The sandy-haired boy nodded. "Oh, yeah. I noticed because the kid—Benji, right?—had a really awesome orange snow jacket. I wanted to ask him where he got it."

"That's him!" I clapped a hand to my heart. "Oh my God. When did you see him?"

"Did they go into the pharmacy?" Mila added.

"It was like two hours ago," the sandy-haired boy replied. "Not sure if they went inside or not. They seemed to be arguing about something."

"You didn't see the posters?" Mila said. "Or inform the police?"

The boy eyeballed the nearest poster. "Lady, no offense, but that poster could be a lost dog sign for all I know. I thought the guy was his dad or something. It didn't look suspicious."

"What about the man?" I asked. "What did he look like?"

The boy shrugged. "He looked nice. Not creepy

or anything. Kinda average. Brown hair, I think. I don't really remember."

I clapped the boy on the shoulder. "Thank you so much. You have no idea how much you've helped us. Mila, let's check the pharmacy."

The pharmacy, like every other business in Wolf Park, was locally owned. From the outside, it looked more like a tacky gift shop where tourists could pick up key chains and sunscreen than a place for buying medications. Wind chimes and dream catchers decorated the windows. I skirted several racks of tie-dye T-shirts with Wolf Park Ski Resort emblazoned across the front to reach the front door.

Snacks, common first aid items, and knit hats lined the shelves. The actual pharmacy hid in the back corner of the store, with nothing to identify its professionalism other than the man in the white coat behind the counter. As we approached, he sorted pills into a bottle.

"Be with you in a moment," he called.

Mila flashed her badge. "How about you be with us now?"

The pharmacist glanced at the badge and immediately stepped away from what he was doing. "How can I help you ladies?"

I flashed the picture of Benji. "We're looking for

this boy. He's eight years old, wearing a bright orange coat. We have reason to believe he might have come into your pharmacy with an older man."

The pharmacist pursed his lips. "I don't believe I've seen that boy. I would have remembered an orange coat. It's my son's favorite color."

My heart dropped. "What about the man? Middle-aged, brown hair?"

"I'm afraid that describes over half the men who come in here," he replied apologetically. "Is there anything else I can do for you?"

"Has anyone requested insulin from you?" Mila asked. "In the last few hours, I mean."

"Several people," the pharmacist said. "I have quite a few patients with insulin needs. At least four of them picked up their prescriptions today."

"What about someone without a prescription?" I said.

He wrinkled his nose. "I cannot legally provide medication to anyone without a prescription. Should I be worried? Do you think someone's stolen from me?"

"Check your insulin stock," Mila ordered. "Do you have security cameras around the pharmacy?"

The pharmacist disappeared between the shelves to do as Mila commanded. "There's one right outside the front door, but I don't service it much.

Wolf Park doesn't have much trouble with crime. I've never had a break-in before."

"I'd like to see the surveillance video from this morning," Mila replied.

"Certainly." He returned to the front counter. "My insulin is all accounted for. If you'll follow me, the security videos feed to the computer in my office."

He placed a small sign—*back in five minutes*—on the counter and beckoned for us to follow him. On the other side of a storage room stocked with more t-shirts was a small office with mounds of paperwork piled on the desk and a computer that looked older than Ophelia.

The pharmacist shook the mouse to wake up the screensaver. "Let's see. Where are those video files? Ah, here we are."

He clicked on a nameless file and pulled up a video feed. The screen was completely black, except for a small blinking box in the middle that read *Memory full.*

Mila's teeth clenched. "Goddamn it."

"I'm so sorry, ladies," the pharmacist said. "Like I said, I don't keep up with the security."

"You need to," I barked. "For public safety at the very least."

He nodded emphatically. "I'll update the system. I promise. And if I see or hear anything about your missing child, I will inform you immediately. Do you have a card?"

As Mila gave him her professional information, my phone buzzed in my pocket. I answered quickly.

"Hello?"

"Hey, Mom."

"Ophelia? Is everything okay? Where are you?"

"I'm fine," she said quickly. "I've been looking around the resort for Benji, like Mila asked. No luck so far. I want to take a nap, but I lost my room key."

"Go to the front desk and ask for another one."

"I tried," she replied. "They said they need your ID to issue another key card."

"Damn, okay. We're on our way."

8

Mila dropped me off at the resort and made a u-turn to continue scoping the area for Benji. Inside, I found Ophelia leaning against the front desk, making faces at the receptionist when she wasn't looking. When Ophelia spotted me, she let out an exaggerated sigh.

"Thank God," she said, dropping her arms dramatically. "They won't let me into the room without you. Excuse me, receptionist lady?"

The receptionist bristled. "I have a name."

Ophelia squinted at her name time. "Linda? That's pretty. Can you give me a new key card now? My mom's here."

I stepped forward and handed my driver's license to Linda. "Hi, I'm Carolina Caccia. Sorry about the trouble."

Linda struggled not to roll her eyes as she looked me up in the system. "It's nothing to worry about. We can easily get you a new key card."

"You didn't say that half an hour ago," Ophelia muttered murderously.

"We need ID to prove the room is yours," Linda explained. "It's for safety."

"Meanwhile, I'm exhausted, my socks are wet, and I have to pee," Ophelia complained. "All because you didn't believe who my mom was."

"There's a bathroom across the lobby," Linda said.

"Give her a break, O," I ordered. "She's just doing her job."

Linda scanned a fresh room key and handed it over the desk. "It's a five-dollar fee for misplacing the first one."

I dragged Ophelia to the desk. "Get your wallet out, kid."

EVERY TIME I returned to our resort room, I held out hope that Benji would be sitting in the armchair, gazing through the window in search of a new bird. Ophelia would tackle him and noogie him until his head was sore. I would hug him and not let go. That was all I wanted.

Alas, when Ophelia swiped her new key card and

opened the door, the room was empty. Ophelia's dirty clothes from last night lay limply over the armchair. No Benji in sight. I sighed heavily.

Ophelia shed her jacket and made a point of hanging it on the hooks behind the door. Then she kicked off her boots and lined those up along the wall. She stripped off her wet socks and lay them along the window sill to dry in the sun. On a normal day, she would have tossed everything into a messy pile for me to sort out later, but everything was different without Benji. Ophelia, for one thing, was well-behaved.

"I'm starving," Ophelia declared. "Can we order room service?"

"You were out all morning," I said. "I gave you money for food. Why didn't you buy lunch?"

"The cafeteria on the slopes has terrible food," she replied. "The special today was meatloaf. Meatloaf! It's worse than the school lunch."

"I like the food on the slopes," I said. "We're not ordering room service. It's too expensive. Eat your leftovers from last night's dinner. I put them in the mini fridge."

Ophelia trudged to the fridge and pulled it open. I picked up Benji's pillow and pressed it to my face. It didn't smell like him anymore. Other than his suitcase, all evidence of his existence had faded from the room.

"Hey, Mom?"

"Ophelia, we are not ordering room service," I said again. "I don't care if you hate microwaved food—"

"No, it's not that." She took a small box out of the fridge. "Were these Benji's insulin cartridges?"

"Yes, he should have a few left."

She tilted the box to show me inside. "They're gone."

I seized the box to check for myself then peered into the fridge. I shuffled food and drinks around, searching for Benji's extra insulin cartridges. "They have to be here somewhere. Where could they have gone?"

Ophelia got out of my way, brow furrowing as she visually combed the room. "Something's different," she murmured as I continued to frantically search the fridge. "What's different?"

I watched her over the top of the fridge door as she took careful steps around the room. Near Benji's suitcase, she knelt down and picked something up.

"Mom?"

I rushed over. "What is it?"

She handed me a sheet of paper. The jagged edge nicked my finger and drew blood. Sucking on the fresh cut, I brought the paper closer to my face. It had been torn from Benji's new scrapbook, which had disappeared with him. Upon it, someone had drawn a strange figure with abnormally long limbs.

"That's Benji's drawing," Ophelia declared. "I'd recognize his style anywhere."

"Is it?" I asked. "This is different than anything I've seen him draw. Is it one of those weird demon trees?"

She squinted at the paper. "No, but it's definitely his drawing. I can tell from the way he pressed the pencil so hard against the sketchbook."

I glanced around the room, looking for other clues. "Was this here before? Did he drop this before he disappeared?"

"I've been staring at Benji's stuff for, like, three days," Ophelia said, shaking her head. "I definitely didn't see that drawing before."

"Could it have fallen out of his suitcase?"

"Mom, think about it," she replied. "He carried that sketchbook with him everywhere. He hasn't put it down since you gave it to him. Plus, he never rips stuff out of his books unless he wants to give his drawings to someone."

My brain refused to put two and two together. I stared at Ophelia blankly.

"He's been in here, Mom," she said. "Benji came in the room, got his insulin, and dropped the drawing. Nothing else makes sense."

. . .

MILA RETURNED to the resort within ten minutes of my call. She swept our room with an eye as keen as a hawk's, looking for anything else that seemed suspicious or out of place. She barraged us with questions. Did we notice if Benji's insulin was there that morning? What time did Ophelia misplace her keycard? Were any of Benji's other things missing?

Upon further inspection, we discovered two pairs of Benji's jeans, two sweaters, and several pairs of socks and underwear had vanished from his suitcase. But whoever had taken them went to the painstaking trouble of staging everything to look untouched. If Ophelia hadn't noticed the missing insulin or Benji's drawing, I never would have known someone had been in the room.

"You need to switch rooms," Mila advised as she rushed me and Ophelia to the security office. "It's not safe where you are."

"But it was Benji!" Ophelia said. "He came to get his things! No one else would have left that drawing."

"If it was *just* Benji, he would have stayed," Mila said. "My guess is whoever's keeping him didn't want a dead kid on their hands when Benji ran out of insulin. No, it's dangerous for you to stay there."

"What if he comes back?" Ophelia whined. "And he can't find us?"

"That's what I'm here for," Mila said. "I won't let anything happen to Benji."

Shock kept me quiet. Had Benji really been so close? The timing was so wrong. If only I had slept in that morning or agreed with Petra to stay out of the investigation, I might have been in the room when Benji—or whoever accompanied him—came to retrieve his things. My fingers held so tightly to his drawing that I crumpled the page. At the very least, I had proof he was still alive. I couldn't let go of that.

When Mila rapped on the door to the security office, Bo answered.

"Ophelia," she said, completely ignoring me and Mila. "I was hoping I'd seen you soon. I've got something for you."

"Is it a pair of handcuffs?" Ophelia guessed.

Bo chuckled. From a drawer in her desk, she produced a plain digital point-and-shoot camera. "It's for you to give to your brother when you find him. It's not as good as the one you stole, and it's used, but it'll get the job done."

Ophelia examined the camera and took an experimental photo. "Thanks. Benji will be excited."

"Speaking of Benji," Mila said, stepping in front of Ophelia. She showed Bo her badge. "I'm Agent Mila Valdez with the FBI. I'm in charge of Benji's case. We have reason to believe he or his captor returned to the room earlier today. Can I have a look at your security tapes?"

Bo gestured for us to come in. "By all means, make yourself comfortable. God knows the rest of Wolf Park PD already has."

"What do you mean?" I asked.

Bo nodded deeper into the security office. "See for yourselves."

Past Bo's desk, a group of police officers sat around a single computer monitor. Detective Petra Lee controlled the mouse. When she saw us, her ever-lasting frown deepened.

"What are you three doing in here?" she asked. "This is a private area. Employees only."

"You're not an employee," Ophelia shot back.

"I am a police detective," Petra replied childishly. "I can go wherever I want."

Mila shoved her way to the front of the group of police officers. "So can I. Get out of my way. This is federal business."

Petra stood her ground and remained seated in front of the computer. "Whatever information you have, you're obligated to share with me."

"I certainly am not!"

"Do you want to find Benji or not?"

Mila glanced at me. I nodded.

"Fine," Mila grumbled. "Someone entered Carolina's room this morning between the hours of eight and twelve. Benji's clothes and insulin have gone missing. In addition, we found a drawing of his that hadn't been there before. I'd like to review the security tapes to determine who entered the room without permission."

Petra glared at Mila and crossed her arms. "How could anyone have gotten into the room without a key?"

"I lost my key," Ophelia supplied. "Although I'm starting to wonder if someone swiped it from me."

"Unlikely," Petra said. "Did Benji have a key?"

"I think he lost it. But he was with me the entire time."

"Except for when he disappeared."

"I love when you play the blame game," I said in a falsely sweet voice.

Petra smiled, but her eyes remained cold. "I'll be happy to have a look at the tapes."

"Not without me," Mila said.

"Of course," Petra agreed. "But Ophelia and Miss Caccia need to leave."

Ophelia's jaw dropped. "What? We're related to him!"

"Exactly," Petra said. "You could see something on these videos that might upset you and cloud your judgement. I can't have that."

"You're a real piece of work," Mila told Petra.

"I do what I have to do for the sake of keeping

things professional."

"It's fine," I heard myself say. I linked my arm through Ophelia's. "We'll wait outside."

"We will?" Ophelia hissed.

"We will." To Mila, I added, "Keep me posted."

WHILE OPHELIA PACED around the enormous fountain and vehemently swore, I stared at Benji's drawing and attempted to interpret it. It was nothing like his delicate bird or fox pictures with such pretty details and handwritten notes about the species. The pencil gouged the paper, leaving deep indentations. The lines were thick and violent, scribbled in haste. The drawing itself spoke of fear and danger. The figure Benji had outlined was tall and thin, with horrible dark eyes and strangely long legs that bent at horrific angles. Were it not for Ophelia's input, I would never had guessed Benji drew it at all.

"Who does she think she is?" Ophelia said, throwing her hands in the air. "We're Benji's family! We're the ones who found out someone broke into the room! And she blames me for losing the key card when someone obviously *stole* it? Mom, are you even listening to me?"

"Mila will tell us whatever Petra doesn't want us to know," I reminded Ophelia for the tenth time. "That's why I asked her to work the case."

"That's not the point. It's the principle of the thing. It's Petra's audacity." Ophelia flipped her hair out of her face. "I need a donut. Do you want one?"

"No, thank you."

"I'm going to raid the breakfast buffet," she said. "If you're nice to the clean-up ladies, they give you whatever's left."

"Come right back," I ordered. "I can't deal with two missing kids."

Not long after Ophelia left, Mila emerged from the security office. I shot to my feet.

"Well?" I demanded. "What did you find?"

"The only person who went into your room today was the maid," Mila reported. "The video doesn't show Benji or anyone else in the hallway outside your room."

My ribs clenched around my heart. "That doesn't make any sense. Someone must have taken the insulin."

"Petra thinks you misplaced it."

"*What?* Is she nuts?"

Mila placed a hand on her arm to calm me. "Don't worry. I'm on it. We already located the maid who tended to your room. We'll pull her in for questioning to ask about the insulin and Benji's clothes."

"I assume Petra won't let me sit in on that either," I guessed.

Mila shot me a knowing look.

"I figured as much."

W*AIT WAS A FOUR LETTER WORD.* I waited for Ophelia to come back with her donuts. I waited for Petra to leave the resort. I waited for Mila to return from the police department, where they were performing the maid's casual interrogation. Because of Petra, everything had to be above board. Way above board.

By the time Mila returned, Ophelia and I had switched rooms. Because of our trauma, the resort had upgraded us to one of the private cabins for our last night at Wolf Park. Ophelia curled up in a knitted blanket, cradling a cup of hot chocolate as she warmed her feet by the fire. If Benji were here, he'd be inspecting the stuffed birds on the mantel, trying to figure out if they were real or not. Despite the cabin's warmth, nothing felt cozy without my son there.

A soft knock echoed on the door, and I pushed the curtains aside to find Mila waiting on the front step. I let her in.

"What did the maid say?"

She stomped her boots and stepped over the threshold. "I could use a cup of that hot chocolate. Preferably with a shot of Kahlua in it."

"So it's bad news?"

As Mila shook off her jacket, I poured more milk

into the pot and turned the stove back on. She brushed snow from her hair and sat next to Ophelia by the fire. Ophelia propped her feet in Mila's lap as if the older woman was her long-lost aunt. Without hesitation, Mila began to rub Ophelia's calves.

"The maid's name was Ella Smart," Mila reported. "She's a fairly new employee, terrified of being fired. She claims she knows nothing about Benji's clothes or the missing insulin. She went in, cleaned, changed your sheets, and left."

"That's bogus!" Ophelia said before I could reply. "If she's the only person who went into our room this morning, she *must* have stolen Benji's things!"

"I agree," Mila replied, rubbing her eyes. "But since we can't pinpoint the exact time the insulin disappeared, we can't prove the maid did anything."

I stirred a clump of cocoa into the warm milk and willed my anger not to bubble over. "Maids are fired for lesser things, like missing laptops or phones. I want this woman gone."

"We can't do anything about it," Mila said. "But *you* can. Go to the resort and file a complaint against Ella Smart. Maybe that'll encourage her to come forward with the truth."

I poured the hot chocolate into a clean mug, added a shot of vodka, and handed it to Mila. "I'm out of Kahlua. Can you watch Ophelia for a few minutes?"

Mila sighed into her beverage and settled into the sofa. "You got it."

I BUNDLED up and walked the short path to the main resort. For a brief moment, I let myself pretend everything was okay. Benji and Ophelia waited for me in the cabin. We would watch a movie together, curl up in bed, and head home tomorrow. Together.

The peaceful thought got me as far as the lobby before determination and "mom attitude" kicked in. I stalked toward the front desk. Linda, not quite finished with her shift yet, shrank in her seat.

"Can I help you?" she asked in a tiny voice.

"Yes, I want the maid who serviced our room today fired," I declared. "Her name is Ella Smart. I don't care what she says. She's the only person who went into our room today, and things went missing after she left. If I have to call corporate—"

"One second, Miss Caccia." Linda typed furiously on her computer and peered at the screen. "That's what I thought. We don't appear to have anyone named Ella Smart working for our resort."

"I'm sorry?"

"We don't have a maid named Ella Smart," Linda clarified, though I had understood her perfectly the first time. "There's no record of her in our system."

"Then who the hell cleaned my room today?"

Linda picked up the phone and dialed a short number. "Bo, we have a security issue at the front desk. Please advise."

Fuming, I dialed Mila's number.

"Everything okay?" she answered.

"No," I spat. "Ella Smart is not a maid here, Mila. The resort doesn't have her information."

Something crashed on the other end of the line, and Ophelia swore.

"Shit," Mila said. "I dropped my cocoa. Carolina, I have to call Petra. We'll put a BOLO out on the maid and bring her back in. She won't get away with this."

"How did you miss this?" I cried. "You didn't ask for her employee ID?"

"She had one," Mila said. "I'm sorry. Carolina, I'm so sorry. I'll fix this. I promise. I have to go. I'll call you as soon as I know something."

THE NIGHT PASSED IN TENSION. I let Ophelia watch TV until she finally drifted off to sleep, muttering about Benji unwittingly. At some point, I joined her, because I woke at dawn with a crick in my neck that threatened to unravel what was left of my sanity, patience, and hope.

Today, we had to check out of Wolf Park. Today, we would head home. Without Benji.

9

Home was not home without Benji. The house wept over his absence. Dust settled on the things in his room. A pile of his laundry sat on the floor next to the washer because I couldn't bring myself to run the load. Our local pharmacy called; Benji's insulin had automatically been refilled, and it was time to pick it up. The cartridges occupied the same space in the fridge door as they always had, except Benji wasn't here to use them.

Though I tried to hide it from Ophelia, I was falling apart. I suffered from crying spells. They hit me out of nowhere, when something of Benji's popped up without warning. I found a pair of his little boxers under the sink in the bathroom and had a ten-minute meltdown. A few hours later, I realized it was time for his afternoon snack but he wasn't here to eat it. Meltdown number two commenced.

Whenever Ophelia walked into the room, I wiped my eyes and hitched a smile on my face. She pretended not to notice I'd been crying, either out of respect or because she had been sobbing a lot lately too. Since arriving home, the two of us had retreated to our separate corners of the house, no longer confined to the small space of a hotel room.

When she went out, I followed her. I offered to drive her and her friends to the movies. I offered to pick them up. I sat in the gas station parking lot across the street and watched through the windshield as she ate ice cream at Dairy Queen. When she rode her bike to the library, I gave her a two-minute head start before hopping in the car and driving after her. I had one kid left to protect, and I refused to let her out of my sight for more than sixty seconds.

Mila texted or called me almost every hour. When they lost the maid, her and Petra dropped the rivalry between them and began working together. The BOLO had done nothing. Ella Smart, if that was even her real name, had disappeared without a trace. The other maids claimed to know nothing about her, though one admitted someone had stolen her entire cleaning cart while she was busy in another room. Additionally, another guest had found Ophelia's stolen room key outside the women's locker room in the gym. Ella Smart, the fake maid, knew more than she'd let on. Was she the one who had kidnapped Benji?

The following Monday, Ophelia and Benji were due to return to school. Before I became the most paranoid parent on the planet, they both rode the bus. That morning, I knocked on Ophelia's door and offered to drive her instead.

Still in bed, she narrowed her eyes at me. "Why?"

"You hate the bus," I reminded her. "You're always saying it smells and the other kids are too loud."

"Yeah," she agreed. "And you always tell me to suck it up because you don't have time to drive me before work."

"My spring semester doesn't start until tomorrow." I went to her closet and pulled out pieces of an outfit for her. "Which means you're in luck."

"I'm not going to wear that," she declared of the blouse I'd set on her bed. "And those jeans don't fit me anymore."

I held up the pants with the embroidered flower on the back pocket. "I thought these were your favorite."

"Not since fifth grade."

"Well, that was only three years ago."

"Three and a half."

"Whatever." I tossed the jeans at her. "Get dressed. You're going to be late."

Ophelia's morning routine often included a spat with Benji over almost anything: who poured the milk in their cereal first, which one of them got the last frozen toaster waffle, or if Benji could borrow Ophelia's black hat because he'd left his at school and it was too cold to go without one.

Today, it was quiet. Ophelia ate her breakfast in gloomy silence. She reached for the last Pop Tart and slid it into the front pocket of her backpack without a fight. She put on her hat and her boots, staring wistfully at Benji's spare coat in the closet by the door. When I handed her the keys, she warmed up the car and scraped the ice off the windshield without complaint. This time, she extended the handle and got all the ice in the middle too.

"You know," she said, gazing through the window as I drove to school. "I used to wish I was an only child when Benji was younger." She laughed derisively. "Be careful what you wish for, right?"

I reached for her shoulder, but she shrugged it away. "Ophelia, you know this isn't your fault, right? Every older sibling wishes the younger one would vanish every once in a while. You didn't make this happen."

"It feels like I did," she mumbled. "I should have gone with Benji when he left the restaurant."

"Then maybe you would have been taken too," I said. "And I'd have lost both my kids. I can't stand that idea."

"How are you keeping it together?" she asked. "I hear you crying at night. Then you have the strength to follow me and my friends around everywhere we go." When I feigned ignorance of this, she added, "I'm not stupid. I've seen your car parked at the Dairy Queen."

"Sorry, kid," I said. "I'm just worried. As far as keeping it together, I'm doing my best. I've seen parents who fall apart when this happens to their kids. It doesn't help. I have to stay strong and keep believing Benji will come home."

"What if he doesn't?"

My teeth clicked together. "I can't think about that or I *will* fall apart."

AFTER DROPPING OPHELIA OFF, I went to the elementary school down the street, parked, and ambled into the front office.

"Hi, Jill," I greeted the receptionist.

"Carolina," Jill replied happily. "How was your winter break? Did Benji enjoy his ski trip? It was all he could talk about before school let out."

I leaned heavily on the counter. "Actually, that's what I wanted to talk to you about. Benji won't be coming to school today. He's, um, missing."

Jill's perfectly plucked brows knitted together. "He's missing? From where?"

"From me," I replied. My throat tightened, and I felt the tears building again. "He disappeared while we were in Wolf Park. I'm not sure when he'll get back to school."

Jill's own eyes filled with moisture. "Oh. Oh, my goodness. You must be devastated, you poor thing." She came out from behind the desk and embraced me. "I'll let his teachers know. Don't you worry about a thing here."

"Actually, is Miss Franco available?" I asked, sniffling. "I was hoping to talk to her."

"Benji's homeroom teacher? Sure, let me check."

Since the elementary schoolers came in later in the morning, Miss Franco did not have a class to watch over yet. I met her in her classroom, where more things reminded me of Benji: the name tag on his desk, his red-yellow-green clothespins that signified how well he behaved that day, and a bird drawing hung on the cork board at the back of the room.

Miss Franco was younger than me, a fresh-faced twenty-five-year-old with no children of her own. She had the perfect happy-go-lucky attitude and high-pitched voice to work with second graders and the bad habit of speaking to parents the same way.

"I'm so sorry to hear about Benji," she said in a tone that sounded downright cheerful. "I really can't believe something like this would happen. What can I do to help?"

My legs wobbled, so I sat in a tiny chair meant for a child. "I wanted to ask you about Benji. The detective working his case believes he might have run away, but he wasn't exhibiting any signs at home that he was unhappy. How was he doing in class?"

Miss Franco blinked rapidly. "You haven't received any of my calls, have you?"

"What calls?"

"I've attempted to contact you many times regarding Benji's behavior in class," she replied. "I was hoping to set up a parent-teacher conference, but you never got back to me. I even sent home a note on Benji's progress report."

"I never got any calls," I said, confused. "And I didn't see Benji's progress report at all."

She opened a filing cabinet next to her desk, shuffled through it, and extracted a green folder. She skimmed through the paperwork inside. "Here we go. This is the number I've been leaving messages at."

I glanced at it and groaned. "That's my home

number. I never answer because of how many telemarketers call. The answering machine is full."

Miss Franco made a noise of disapproval at the back of her throat. "I'll have to get your cell number then."

"What did I miss?" I asked quickly. "Is Benji doing poorly?"

"His grades are technically fine," she assured me. "Though he has been scoring on the lower end of my scale. Unfortunately, his behavior in class is quite worrying."

"His behavior? He's the quietest kid I've ever met."

"He used to be," Miss Franco said. "But over the last few months, Benji's grown erratic. He gets frustrated easily. I've had to send him outside on multiple occasions for disrupting the class."

"How has he been disrupting?"

"Screaming, crying, throwing himself on the floor," she replied. "It's the kind of behavior I expect to see from my kindergarteners, not my second graders. I suspected something might be wrong at home."

I swallowed the lump in my throat. "Nothing's changed in a while. His dad—it's complicated, but I can't think of why he would suddenly behave so poorly."

"You hadn't noticed anything at home?"

"No, he's been fine."

"He excels in art," Miss Franco said, as if this were some kind of consolation prize. "He draws exceedingly well. However, he also draws during other classes. When I ask him to pay attention to the task at hand, it triggers another meltdown."

I dropped my head and kneaded my temples. "I can't believe I missed this. I have to call Petra and let her know she was right. God, I hate that."

Miss Franco cleared her throat. "What was that?"

"Sorry," I said, straightening up. "I realized I don't know my son as much as I thought I did. He never told me he was having problems in class."

"I'll keep extra copies of the lessons and homework we do," she offered. "When he returns—and I expect him to return—he can take all the time he needs to catch up."

My chin trembled as the familiar wave of almost-tears washed over me. I quickly stood and shook Miss Franco's hand. "Thank you for everything. I promise I'll be more involved with Benji's education in the future if—*when* he gets back."

As soon as I exited the classroom, I lost it in the hallway. Big, fat, ugly sobs. Salty tears burned the dried corners of my eyes and the skin around my nose and lips. I blotted my face with a Dairy Queen napkin and got ahold of myself as I walked to the car. There, I dialed a number I never thought I'd dial.

"Detective Lee?"

"This is she," Petra replied curtly. "May I ask who's calling?"

"It's Carolina Caccia," I said. "I wanted to let you know. I went to Benji's school and spoke to his homeroom teacher. Apparently, he's been acting out in class over the last several months."

A pen scratched against paper as Petra scribbled notes. "Details?"

"He's been throwing temper tantrums," I continued. "The teacher says he's unable to focus unless he's drawing. She's had to send him outside multiple times."

"You weren't aware of any of this?"

"We had a miscommunication," I replied, "and Benji seemed fine at school."

She didn't say *I told you so*, but I could hear it in her tone when she replied.

"You do realize what this means, correct?" she asked.

"It's more evidence that he ran away," I said robotically.

Petra sighed wistfully. "Miss Caccia, I do not take pleasure in being right in these scenarios. Do you understand that?"

"Not quite."

"My greatest wish is to reunite you and your son," she said. "Thank you for calling me. Since I have you, I'd like you to know we're doing everything we can to locate Benji. I've ordered an aerial search of Wolf Park and the surrounding counties. We've got Ella Smart's license plate number in the system, so we're looking for her car. I promise I am working as hard as I can to get Benji back safely, whether he ran away or he was taken."

"Thank you," I muttered. "Thank you, Detective Lee."

"You can call me Petra."

When I arrived home, my mother's car was parked in the driveway. I steeled myself for what waited inside. She accosted me as soon as I came in through the garage door.

"Why didn't you tell me you were back?" she demanded, holding a broom in one hand and a mop in the other as if she had the power to complete both tasks at once. "This place is an absolute wreck! No wonder Benji disappeared! Who would want to live in this pig sty?"

I pushed past her to hang my purse on the coat hook behind the door. "What are you doing here, Mother?"

"Someone has to take care of you and Ophelia."

She followed me with the broom, mopping slush and dirt off the floor as it came off my shoes. "Where are your house slippers? I thought I taught you better than to wear your shoes inside. It spreads all kinds of germs. Not good for children."

"My slippers are in the wash."

"I'll get you a pair of thick socks to wear instead. Take off those boots."

Before I had the chance, she knelt down, undid the laces, and carried my shoes to the mat by the front door. Then she disappeared upstairs, presumably to look for socks.

"Well?" she demanded as she peeled off my wet socks and replaced them with thick fuzzy ones she'd bought for my birthday the year before. "Any news on Benji?"

"No. They're doing an aerial search for him now."

She scoffed. "That won't help if he's in Amos's house."

"What are you talking about?"

Mom opened the pantry and took items out at random. "I have a hunch. I think Amos is rethinking the custody agreement. He took Benji out of revenge. Benji was always his favorite. He never cared much for Ophelia—"

"Mom, stop."

"What? It's true."

"I meant stop emptying my pantry." I pushed

pasta, cereal, and a new box of Pop Tarts across the counter for her to put away again. "But you can also stop speculating about Amos. He doesn't have Benji, and he loves Ophelia."

"Oh, really? Where's the proof?" She tossed her hands in the air. "What the hell? Let's go to his house right now. I bet we find Benji locked in a linen closet."

She strolled out of the kitchen, grabbed her coat, and took my car keys.

"What are you doing?" I demanded.

"Are you deaf?" she asked. "We're going to Amos's to see if Benji is there."

"Are you insane?"

"It's debatable. Come on. Put on your shoes and coat. Change out of those socks. They won't keep your feet warm if they get wet."

I TOLD myself I got in that car with my mother to stop her from doing something crazy, but if I was honest, I also wanted to know what Amos's new life with Pilar looked like on the inside. They lived a mere five miles from us. Ophelia and Marin went to the same high school. Nessa and Benji were zoned for the same middle school next year.

"Ridiculous," Mom muttered as I pointed out

Pilar's house. "Not even a ten-minute drive from his old house. That man has nerve."

"Okay, you've seen the place" I said. "Can we go now?"

"Of course not. We're checking inside."

"What—Mom, no!"

She put the car in park and got out, ignoring me. I followed hastily. Pilar's house was a little larger than ours. It had a balcony on the front that looked out on the rest of the neighborhood. A white curtain covered the French doors that no doubt led to the master bedroom. Up there, Amos had fallen in love with a new woman.

Mom knocked impatiently and planted her hands on her waist. Pilar's curious face appeared in the window. When she saw us, she turned her confusion into a smile.

"Hello," she said, beckoning us over the threshold. "Come on in. I wasn't expecting you. Have you heard any news on Benji?"

"Not yet," I replied. "Sorry for barging in. We just—"

"Where's Amos?" Mom demanded, stalking past Pilar.

"He's at work," she said. "You must be Carolina's mother. I don't believe we've officially met. I'm Pilar."

"I know who you are," my mother replied, ignoring Pilar's outstretched hand. "I'm Lina."

"Oh, like your nickname?" Pilar asked me. "That's lovely that you're named after your mother."

"It's tradition," Mom said. "Or it was until Amos came along. What kind of name is Ophelia anyway?"

"I picked Ophelia actually," I told her. "You know that."

Mom huffed and moved farther into Pilar's house, examining the flowery wallpaper and the kids' class pictures on the wall. "You don't mind if we look around, do you, Pilar?"

Pilar gestured for her to continue. "Not at all."

As my mother checked every nook and cranny with an air of determination, Pilar led me into the kitchen and poured a cup of tea.

"I'm so sorry," I said again. "She's crazy. She thinks Amos kidnapped Benji, and I couldn't convince her otherwise. She's going to search your entire house."

Pilar waved dismissively. "I understand. She doesn't know me. Let her look, if it makes her feel better." She added honey to the cup of tea and pushed it toward me. "What about you? What would make you feel better?"

"Finding Benji," I said. "That's all I want."

"I can't help you do that," she said. "But I can make you dinner. Why don't you stay?"

"No, I couldn't impose," I said hurriedly. "Plus I have my mother with me, and I need to pick up Ophelia from school."

Pilar took out her phone. "I'll tell Marin to bring Ophelia home on the bus with her, and your mother is more than welcome to stay too."

10

"I'm home! Wow, something smells delicious. Did you make paella again—?"

Amos stopped short as he rounded the corner into the kitchen and spotted all of us—his ex-wife, his daughter, his current wife, his stepdaughters, and his ex-mother-in law—sitting at the dinner table with our own plates of yellow rice, chicken, shrimp, and vegetables. Pilar and I each nursed a glass of wine. My mother drank bourbon. Ophelia happily sipped on two percent milk with Marin and Nessa, a remarkable feat when she usually fought me for soda every night.

Amos dropped his keys in a bowl on the kitchen counter and warily gazed around. "What exactly is happening here?"

"We decided to have dinner together," Pilar

answered simply. She stood, kissed Amos's cheek, and offered him a plate. "Come sit, honey."

Amos took the empty seat at the head of the table, between me and Pilar. He leaned toward me and, under his breath, said, "Did you set this up?"

"I did not," I replied. "Mom was being—well, Mom—and she invited herself over here. Pilar was kind enough to let us stay. I wasn't going to accept, but Ophelia needed this."

Amos glanced at his collective group of daughters. Ophelia and Marin laughed at a funny face Nessa made. Across the table, Pilar engaged my mother in an emphatic conversation about the annual need to clean out your dryer vents. Amos lifted an eyebrow.

"This is not what I expected when I got remarried," he admitted in a low tone.

"It's all down to Pilar," I said. "I was determined to hate her, but I can't. She's too good a person. You married a better woman."

"Don't say that," he said, and I was surprised by the amount of offense in his voice. "Don't compare yourself to Pilar. You have different ambitions and priorities. That's all. No one is better than the other."

I studied the earnestness of his expression. "You're different too. I noticed during the ski trip. I mean, you still screw up. Benji's birthday was a prime example of that, but once you figure out how to balance everything, you'll be great."

He sat a little farther away from me, stunned. "Did you just give me a compliment?"

"I said you *will* be great," I emphasized, going back to my paella. "It's a future compliment. It doesn't count until you fulfill the prophecy."

Amos chuckled, but his eyes didn't shine like they usually did when he laughed.

"What's the matter?" I said.

"You have to ask?" He glanced toward Ophelia, as if to make sure she was busy with her stepsisters before continuing. "This wouldn't be happening if Benji hadn't gone missing, and he's missing because of me."

"That's not true," I said automatically.

"Really?" he asked. "You just said Benji ran away because I screwed up his birthday."

"That's not what I said," I replied, even though I was thinking it.

"You were thinking it."

I shut my mouth.

Amos stabbed a shrimp but didn't eat it. "I want to enjoy this, but I can't without Benji here. It's not the same."

Without thinking, I clasped his hand in mine. He held tightly to my fingers. Pilar's gaze flickered to our interlinked grasp. She smiled and returned to the conversation with my mother.

"We'll find Benji," I promised Amos. "When we do, we'll make sure our family stays together. We had the right idea, going on vacation together, but we'll do better in the future."

He nodded, his eyes bright with moisture. "Are you working with Mila?"

"No, she's in Wolf Park with the detective."

"You backed out of the investigation?"

"I was never a part of the investigation," I reminded him. "You and Petra wanted me to stay out of it."

Amos chewed thoughtfully on his shrimp. "But they haven't made any progress."

"No, they haven't."

"You're a better investigator than Mila."

"We were partners," I said. "We worked well together."

"But she doesn't have you anymore."

"Are you just stating facts?" I asked. "What do you want to know?"

He reached across me to help Nessa cut a larger piece of chicken into smaller bites. "Doesn't it seem odd that neither local or federal investigative services have found a single lead? They must have missed something. *You* wouldn't have missed something."

I scoffed, recalling my later days with the agency, when all of my drama at home affected the quality of my work. "A lot of kids died because I *did* miss something."

"That was because of me," he said. "But if you didn't have all that pressure, you could find Benji."

"I don't know," I said. "He's my son. My viewpoint is skewed. Besides, I don't have the resources that Mila and Petra do. I can't request an aerial search of the state."

"You have a way of getting what you want even if you're not supposed to have it," Amos said wryly. "That's why you called Mila in the first place, isn't it?"

"You know me too well."

"I won't tell you what to do," he said. "I know searching for your own son is a lot different than locating someone else's missing child. It's a conflict of interest. I get that, but I can't help thinking you're the best person for the job."

Pilar interrupted us with another spoonful of paella aimed at my plate. "Eat," she ordered me. "You'll need your strength. Girls, stop playing with the shrimp tails and put them in the garbage."

My mother stood to refill her bourbon. As she opened the fridge for ice cubes, she let out a gasp. "There's insulin in here. You *did* kidnap Benji!"

Amos shot me a warning look, but Pilar easily defused the situation.

"We keep extra insulin in case Benji ever visits," she explained, leading Mom away from the fridge. She refilled Mom's glass and added a touch of ginger ale. "It's a precautionary measure. I was hoping he'd get the chance to spend some time here. I still am."

On the way home, Mom gave Pilar a raving five-star review. Nonstop, she chattered about Pilar's welcoming spirit, her tasty paella, and her keen ability to make everyone feel at home. Ophelia rolled her eyes and put in her headphones. I briefly wished I had the same opportunity.

"I suppose that's it for tonight," Mom said as she pulled into our driveway. She gazed wistfully at the house. "The fun's over. Back to reality."

"Why don't you stay tonight?" I asked. "I can make up the guest room."

She brightened. "Really?"

"Yes. I have to go back to work tomorrow, and I wouldn't mind some help getting Ophelia out of the house in the morning."

"All right." She cheerfully put her car in park and got out. "Are you excited to go back to work?"

I thought of the eager students at the community school where I taught. Each one of them dreamt of a career in law enforcement. None of them knew the risks—emotional, physical, or otherwise—that came with the job.

"Gotta pay the bills," I said to Mom.

My alarm had been going off for five minutes when I finally awoke. My neck ached as I peeled my face from the pillow and swiped across the phone screen to dismiss the annoying sound meant to wake me gently from REM sleep. I caught sight of the time and swore. I hadn't set the right alarm the night before. Ophelia had to leave for school in ten minutes. Otherwise, she'd be late.

I rolled out of bed, stomped into the hallway, and threw open Ophelia's door to find her bed empty. Coldness clamped around my heart. I couldn't possibly have lost both children.

"O?" I called through the house.

"Downstairs!" she shouted back.

Relief warmed my veins as I returned to my room to get my slippers and robe to keep me warm. The fatty smell of bacon and eggs cooked in olive oil floated up the stairs. My mother's and Ophelia's voices gabbed below.

"No, I *don't* like him," Ophelia was saying as I came into the kitchen. She fiercely stabbed a piece of bacon. "Grandma, are you listening to me? He called me a dyke."

"It's probably because he likes *you*," Mom replied as she manned a frying pan on the stove.

"Insulting me and the queer community is not the way to my heart," Ophelia replied. "Also, boys are stupid."

"Hear, hear!" I said, lifting a mug of coffee in solidarity.

"Oh, good. You're awake." Mom filled a clean plate with enough scrambled eggs to choke a horse, several strips of bacon, and a homemade drop biscuit. "Eat this."

"I don't eat breakfast," I said. "Coffee's good."

"That's ridiculous." She steered me toward the island counter and forced me to sit next to Ophelia. "Breakfast is the most important meal of the day. Eat your food."

"I tried to skip too," Ophelia muttered to me. "But she lured me in with the drop biscuits. Can you get the recipe for those?"

"Your mother can't bake," Mom announced. "She burns everything."

"That's not true," I protested. "Fine, it's a little true."

"Teach me to make the biscuits then," Ophelia said. "I want to share them with Benji when he gets home."

Ophelia's newfound optimism felt like a kick in

the pants. If the most nihilistic member of the family could hope for Benji's return, so could I.

"No time to learn biscuit-making now," I said. "You have to get to school. I'll take you."

"No, no." Mom turned off the stove and moved the pan off the heat. "You get ready for work, Carolina. I'll take Ophelia to school."

"Really?" I asked, surprised.

"Of course." She kissed my forehead. "Eat your breakfast and get to work. Don't worry about Ophelia. I've got it handled."

THEY LEFT TWO MINUTES EARLY, which meant Ophelia would be on time to class in the first time since the beginning of the school year. My first class didn't start until eleven, so I had time to shower, get dressed, and steady myself before I drove to the local community college.

On the way there, a new billboard caught my attention. It had my son's face on it, blown up to twenty times its normal size so the whole state of North Carolina could see it. I stared at it for so long that I didn't notice when the light turned green. The person behind me beeped, and I jolted back to reality.

Petra and Mila must have decided to post the billboard. The number printed in big black letters matched the Wolf Park PD telephone line. It meant two things: that they still hadn't had any breakthroughs finding Benji, and they didn't want to admit it to me. I tapped the button on my steering wheel that controlled my car's Bluetooth.

"Call Mila," I said.

"Calling Mila," replied the cool automated car voice.

The line rang for several seconds, and I was sure I'd have to leave a voicemail, but Mila finally answered. "Hey, Carolina. Can you hold on a second?"

"Sure—"

"Don't you dare touch that! That is evidence! I will take your head off if you bring that anywhere else—sorry, Carolina," she added in a less severe tone. "What can I help you with?"

"I saw the billboard."

Her voice grew tight. "Yeah, we're in a spot. We need all the help we can get."

"What did you find?"

"Nothing. That's the problem."

"No, the evidence you were shouting about," I clarified. "What was it?"

"Oh." Mila sighed, and I imagined her rubbing her head with the tips of her fingers like she always did when she was particularly stressed. "Benji doesn't have asthma, does he?"

"No, just diabetes."

"That's what I thought, but we found an albuterol inhaler near where Benji disappeared when we went for another look."

"Someone could have dropped that after the fact," I said. "It doesn't mean it's evidence."

"I know that."

"But you shouldn't discount it."

"I know that too. Can you let me do my job?"

I balked at the sharpness of her question. "First, you want me to butt in. Now you don't? Everyone's playing hot and cold with me."

"Maybe I didn't understand how tough this would be," Mila snapped. "Locating my best friend's missing kid without a single lead? It's not only humiliating, it's devastating. If I don't find Benji, I'm a failure. I'll have failed you, him, the agency, and myself."

"Mila, I—"

"Excuse me, I have to go. We're checking the inhaler for prints."

"*Call ended,*" said the car.

DUE TO HITTING every single red light on the way to campus, I arrived to class late. The students shifted in their chairs and stared at their phones. None of them had bothered to take out pens or paper. They all had laptops for their notes.

"Laptops and phones away," I announced before introducing myself. "If you need to take notes, do it the old-fashioned way. Science says you'll retain information better if you write it down anyway."

The usual groans and glares of annoyance met my attention. I ignored it as I took my place at the desk and shook the school computer awake. As I navigated to my Welcome to Criminology 101 PowerPoint, I felt the students' eyes on me. These first few minutes of meeting a new professor were crucial. Here, they decided whether or not they would make an effort in this class.

"My name is Carolina Caccia," I said. "*Catch-uh.* Don't mispronounce my last name, or I won't bother to answer your questions. This is Criminology 101. Is everyone in right place?"

One student, a girl with a scared look, got up and left.

"One down, twenty-two to go," I joked. No one laughed, so I cleared my throat and pulled up the first page of the PowerPoint. "Anyway, here's a few things about me. Before I turned to the wonderful field of teaching, I worked for the FBI. My specialty was missing children cases. I studied foreign languages as an undergraduate student, gained experience with a private company that sussed out

THE GIRL IN THE SNOW

human trafficking scenarios, then applied for the FBI. After ten years, I retired and decided to teach—"

A kid fresh out of high school with dull brown hair that grew to his shoulders shot his hand up.

"Questions already?" I said. "What's your name?"

"Max," he replied eagerly. "Why did you quit the FBI?"

"It was a personal decision." No way was I going to explain my marriage difficulties to this bunch. "Moving on, this class is to teach the basics of—"

Max's hand hovered in the air again.

"Yes, Max?"

"I don't understand why you would quit the FBI. Isn't it like the pinnacle of investigative work?" Max couldn't remain still in his chair. "Did you get in trouble or something?"

"If you must know, I retired from the agency to take care of my family," I snapped. *"Moving on,* let's take a look at the syllabus. You'll have readings almost every day and quizzes—"

Yet another hand, not Max's this time, went up.

"Yes?" I sighed.

The new interrupter was a young woman who reminded me of Ophelia in looks but certainly not in attitude. "Sorry, but can you tell us what it's like to be in the FBI? I know we're supposed to be going over the syllabus and stuff, but it's so much more interesting to hear what it's *actually* like doing investigative work."

"You want to know what it's like?" I asked.

The class murmured in assent. I clicked out of the PowerPoint, and the screen went black. As I stepped to the center of the room, all eyes followed me.

"Okay, here's the scenario," I said. "A single mother takes her two kids to Wolf Park Ski Resort for a five-day vacation. She has a thirteen-year-old daughter and an eight-year-old son with Type 1 diabetes. There, she meets her ex-husband, his new wife, and their two daughters. On the second night of the trip, her son gets upset at dinner and asks to be excused. The mother agrees, allowing her son to walk back to the resort on his own, but he never makes it back to the room. The mother panics and calls the police. That's you. What's your plan of action?"

"Search the resort," Max answered easily.

"Done," I said. "No sign of the child."

"Interview everyone present at the scene of the crime," another student piped in.

"Also done," I said. "No one saw the child disappear. No one has any information. What now?"

"Get the FBI involved."

I point to the student with this suggestion to indicate the answer is correct. "Good. The case gets registered to a national database, and a special agent is dispatched to the area. Let's call her Agent Black. Agent Black reviews the situation, but she can't discover any leads. The mother has to return home without her child. What now?"

Max wrinkled his nose. "Why would the mother leave the area?"

"She has another child," I reminded the class. "That child has to return to school, the mother has to return to work. They have to go on with their lives."

"That's bullshit," Max declared. "If my kid was missing, I wouldn't go anywhere until I found him. The mom should get someone else to watch her daughter and take a leave of absence from work. That way, she can devote her time to finding her son."

"That's not the way these things work," I replied. "The investigators don't want the mother to get involved with their work."

Max leaned back in his seat. "This mom took her kids on vacation to Wolf Park. She excused her son from dinner when he was upset instead of forcing him to sit there and stew in his emotions. Sounds like a mom with a good head on her shoulders who knows her kids well. If I were the investigator, I'd make the mom my prime source of information."

Something clicked in my mind as Max stretched

his arms overhead. He was saying all the things I had said to Petra in the beginning, except *I* had given up.

"Thank you, Max." I reached for my purse. "On that note, you're all dismissed. I'll email you the syllabus, though I doubt we'll have class until I return from Wolf Park. I'll let the dean know you require someone to teach until I get back."

Stunned, they all watched as I left the classroom with a determined look on my face.

11

It took the rest of the day to sort out my plan. I convinced my mother to stay at my house with Ophelia while I returned to Wolf Park. I gave myself two weeks to find Benji or at least make significant headway on his location. If that time passed without any luck, I would return home to my daughter and hand the investigation back over to Mila and Petra.

I packed my warmest clothes, knowing I'd be on the slopes to look for Benji at some point. I also packed a few things I never did a job without: my watch, a small Moleskin notebook, and a photo keychain. The picture featured fourteen-year-old Jillian Diamond. She was the first kid I ever found during my time with the FBI. I had rescued her from the basement of a registered sex offender, a mere three doors down from her own house. I promised myself I'd never forget the look on Jillian's face when we brought her home. That was the main reason I put myself through hell for this job. These kids deserved to come home.

I didn't tell anyone what I was doing, not even Mom or Ophelia. Ophelia wasn't stupid though. She came into my bedroom as I packed my bag.

"Oh, your lucky keychain," she said, inspecting Jillian's picture. "This girl's, like, in her twenties now, right?"

"Yeah, she'd be twenty-four now." Distracted, I searched the closet for another pair of warm socks. "Are you sure you're going to be okay with Grandma? I'm going to be gone for a while."

"I'll be fine," she promised. "As long as you come back with Benji."

"I didn't say I was going to look for him."

She rifled through my suitcase without permission, messing up my careful organization system. "Why else would you be going back to Wolf Park with all your FBI stuff?"

"What stuff?"

She shot me a wry look. "Whatever you do, can you be careful? Dad used to worry you'd do something stupid and get into trouble. Didn't the agency try to suspend you once or twice?"

"Sometimes, you have to do something stupid to

get your job done," I replied. "The agency respected that."

"I'm not gonna respect it if the dude who took Benji sends you both home in a box," she said bluntly.

"Ophelia!"

"What? You always tell me to say what I feel."

"Within reason," I replied. "And with a tiny bit of tact."

She shrugged. "You never specified before. Anyway, what are you going to do about Mila and Detective Lee? I thought they were blocking you out of the investigation."

"I don't exactly plan on letting them know my intentions."

"You mean you're gonna lie."

"No, I'm going to artfully disguise my truth."

"So you're gonna lie."

I tossed an extra sweater toward the suitcase but purposely aimed for Ophelia. Quick as a flash, she caught it, balled it up, and threw it unceremoniously in with the rest of my clothes.

"Don't cause any trouble for Grandma," I warned her, zipping the suitcase. "Go to school, do your homework, and don't stay out too late. If I get a call that my daughter's gone missing too, I'll lose my mind."

She held up two fingers. "Scout's honor. Weird though, right?"

"What is?"

"You always thought *I'd* be the one to disappear."

***

THE HOUR'S drive to Wolf Park was unusually quiet without my children bickering in the backseat. I never thought I'd miss it, but the silence weighed heavily on my shoulders. Anxiety crept in and made my blood cold, despite the heat pumping through the car vents. Since I couldn't be alone with my thoughts, I dialed Amos. Part of me was disappointed when I got sent to voicemail. The other part was relieved.

"Hey, Amos," I said after the beep. "It's Carolina. I just wanted to let you know I'm taking a short leave of absence from work and heading back to Wolf Park. I want to be there in case Benji shows up. My mom's watching Ophelia, but it'd be great if you or Pilar could check in with her every once in a while. Maybe have her for dinner if that's not too much trouble. I think it's good for her to hang out with Nessa and Marin. Anyway, I'll talk to you soon and—"

The timer on the voicemail cut me off. *"If you would like to re-record your message, please press one. If you're satisfied with your message, please hang up."*

THE GIRL IN THE SNOW

I sighed, hung up, and turned on the radio.

"This one's for all the lost children, wishing them well and wishing them home," Michael Jackson crooned.

"Are you kidding me?" I muttered, switching the station. "That's not even a single. God, play Thriller or something."

AS THE ROAD steeped and the mountains appeared up ahead, a thrill of excitement pumped through my heart. The prospect of finding Benji made me feel useful for the first time in years. I hadn't realized how much joy my old job had brought me. The thrill lay in doing something good and knowing that my job had a positive impact on society. This time around, it was a double whammy. If I did my job right, I'd get my son back too.

My first stop in Wolf Park was the police department. I parked in the corner of the lot and kept an eye on the front door, munching on an egg and cheese bagel from the local cafe as I waited. After an hour or so, Mila and Petra emerged from the station. As usual, they were arguing. Petra gesticulated wildly as they headed toward Mila's car.

"Shut up and get in," Mila said, so forcefully that I heard her through the windows of my van.

Once they were gone, I took my chances. I zipped up my coat and braved the icy walk into the station. Wolf Park PD had a tiny office. The small town didn't warrant much more than a few desks and a cheap coffee maker. No one greeted me at the door, which was all the better for me.

The officers on desk duty didn't glance up from their paperwork as I walked by them. The key to fitting in, I'd learned in the past, was to act like you owned the place. I kept my shoulders squared and my chin high and strolled right into Detective Lee's office. It was easy to find; she was the only person who had an office.

Luckily for me, Petra relied on her incompetent officers to keep nosy people like me out of her office. There was no lock on her door or on the filing cabinet. Naturally, a password protected her computer, but if I had to guess, Petra liked to do things in an old-fashioned kind of way. I pulled open the topmost drawer of the filing cabinet and rifled through it. She'd even found beige folders to store her documents in. Go figure.

Sure enough, she kept everything she had on Benji on paper. I took out the file and hastily flipped through it, taking pictures of each document with my phone. There wasn't much to go on: Benji's hospital records, mine and Amos's descriptions of what happened that night, and several pictures of the spot where he'd disappeared. Petra's handwritten notes didn't help much either. Much of her hunches had been scribbled out, no doubt when she disproved them.

"Not particularly comforting, Detective Lee," I muttered to myself as I put everything back where it belonged. "Now where's your key to the evidence locker?"

I searched the desk drawers and found multiple golden keys strewn about without any labels on them. I took them all and slipped out of Petra's office. In the hall, I had no idea where I was going. It cost me: a female officer with a donut in hand noticed I looked out of place.

"Can I help you?" she said, stopping mid-strut to step into my way.

"Actually, yes," I replied. "Can you point me to the evidence locker? This is my first time here."

She looked me up and down. "Are you an investigator?"

"I'm with the agency," I said. "Working undercover nearby. Don't have my badge on me though."

She wasn't buying it. "If you don't have any identification, I can't let you into the evidence room. You shouldn't be back here at all."

"But I have a key." I held up one of the many golden keys I'd pilfered from Petra's office, hoping it was the right one or at least *looked* like the right one. "How else would I have gotten it?"

The officer narrowed her eyes. "Where *did* you get that?"

"From Petra."

She relaxed. Anyone on a first-name basis with Detective Lee had to be important. She jerked her chin toward the back corner of the department.

"Evidence locker is the last door on the left, past the bathrooms. Special Agent—?"

"Smith," I replied, already on my way past her.

"I'll let Detective Lee know you're here," she called after me.

"Great," I muttered. "She'll be thrilled."

I checked my watch, figuring I had about twenty minutes tops before Petra figured out "Special Agent Smith" was up to no good and turned around to come looking for me. At the door to the evidence locker, I fished all the keys out of my pocket and shoved each one in the knob. After six tries, I finally found one that fit. The knob clicked, and I shoved the door open. Eighteen minutes to find that damned inhaler and get the hell out of here. Plenty of time.

Despite Wolf Park's stellar reputation as a beautiful small town with limited crime, the evidence locker was stocked full of drugs, weapons, and paraphernalia. For the most part, baggies of dried-up marijuana, pot pipes, and bongs lined the shelves. Apparently, the people of Wolf Park really liked to get high, even if recreational weed wasn't legal here yet.

As with all evidence lockers, a few questionable items had been stored here as well, including a lawn gnome with a broken nose, a pair of brand-new noise-cancelling headphones with a spot of dried blood on the earpiece, and a single metal tumbler with the ability to keep your drink cold or hot for hours on end. This one, however, was filled with the burnt ends of joints, or as the stoners called them, "roaches."

"Sheesh," I said to myself, tipping the metal cup toward me to see inside. "There's gotta be hundreds in there. Wonder how long that took to collect."

I returned to the task at hand: finding the inhaler Mila had spoken of, along with whatever other evidence they had collected on Benji's behalf. It wasn't an easy feat. The locker hadn't been organized in years. The officers dumped stuff in here like it was a storage unit. I picked through the bagged items, searching for anything labeled "Benjamin Clark."

"Special Agent Smith? Who the hell is that?"

The harried voice unmistakably belonged to Detective Petra Lee. I let out a colorful swear and checked my watch. Twenty-two minutes had passed without my knowledge. I'd forgotten to keep an eye on the clock. Frantic, I peeked into the hallway.

Petra stood with the officer who had questioned me, hands on her hips. My only escape was the emergency exit at the end of the hallway, which would most definitely trigger an alarm.

"Here goes nothing," I muttered.

Right as I was about to bolt, the corner of a plastic bag on a high shelf caught my eye. I reached up to take it down. The inhaler and the drawing we'd found in our room the night Benji's insulin had gone missing tumbled into my arms. I breathed a sigh of relief. I had the evidence. Now, I just had to get out of here without Petra noticing.

I checked the hallway again. Petra had stormed around the officer and was making a beeline for the evidence locker. My only chance of escape lay in a helpfully placed support pole that held the ceiling up. In a matter of seconds, it would obscure Petra's view of the emergency exit, but I'd only have a few moments to make it out of the building, into my car, and out of the parking lot before the entire department came after me.

Petra stepped behind the support pole.

"Now or never," I told myself and dashed for the exit, drawing up my hood to keep my face away from any cameras.

As soon as I pushed open the door, a stream of sunlight blinded me and the alarm blared overhead. I slammed the door shut and wedged a huge rock in the space beneath it. Then I tucked the baggie of evidence into the front of my coat and ran blindly, starting my car with the remote in my pocket.

I didn't look back as a commotion erupted behind me. Officers pounded on the emergency exit door, but the rock held. No one managed to get out as I leapt into my car and peeled out of the driveway. I'd probably get arrested later—I'm sure the department had cameras covering the parking lot—but if I found Benji, it would all be worth it.

I drove to the resort, told the parking attendant I was checking in, and got a spot near the slopes. As happy people and their children skied and snowboarded without a care in the world, I drew the baggie from my coat to inspect my stolen evidence.

I unfolded Benji's drawing first. A chill crept across my neck like the furry legs of a wolf spider. I rubbed the back of my neck and rolled out my shoulders.

The drawing creeped me out. The figure's treelike limbs and oddly-shaped legs were not humanly proportioned. Benji always focused on reality when he drew. Something like this was out of character for him.

"What are you trying to tell me, buddy?" I murmured, squinting at the violently-drawn lines.

When nothing about the drawing spoke to me, I moved on to the inhaler. I recognized it easily. A lot of people with asthma used the same one, including a few kids from the cases I'd worked in the past. It wasn't exactly a lead; a good portion of the people on the slopes probably had the exact same inhaler in their pockets right now.

Fortunately, the number of the pharmacy that had filled the prescription was taped to the inhaler. I dialed the pharmacy.

"Hi, I'd like to refill a prescription," I said when someone answered the phone. "But I can't find the box for it. Do you already have my information on file?"

"Most likely," the pharmacist answered. "What's the prescription number and patient's date of birth?"

"I have the prescription number, and the birthday is—oh, shoot." I did my best to sound harried and flustered. "I'm so sorry. The patient is my friend's kid. I can't remember her birthday. She's at soccer practice, and her mom asked me to look after her. She really needs her inhaler. Can't you just use the prescription number?"

"Unfortunately, I can't fill the prescription without that information, ma'am. Is there anything I can help you with?"

"Isn't the patient's information already in the system?"

"Yes, but I need you to verbally confirm the name

and birthday," the pharmacist replied. "Otherwise, I don't know if I'm refilling this for the right person."

"But what if it's an emergency?"

"Then I suggest you call emergency services."

"But I—"

A sharp rap on my window made me jump. Mila stood outside my door, and she did not look pleased.

"Thanks for your help," I told the pharmacist, hanging up. I shoved the inhaler into the center console before rolling down the window. "Hi, Mila. I was just about to call you."

"Before or after you got arrested for stealing evidence, breaking into police offices, and interfering with an investigation?" she demanded.

"Boy, that was quick," I commented. "I thought I'd at least have an hour before you caught up with me."

"Hand over the evidence, Carolina. What the hell were you thinking?"

I bagged the inhaler and the drawing and gave them to Mila. "I needed to see that inhaler for myself."

"You didn't trust me to keep you updated on Benji's case?" The hurt was evident in her voice.

"You seemed aggravated the last time we talked."

"Because I can't find your kid," she said. "And I can't face you until I do."

"I'm here to help," I told her. "You said it yourself.

We made the best team. I bet we still do. Tell me what I can do to help."

She slumped against the side of my car. "Carolina, I've told you everything I know. We're at a stalemate. If you want to conduct your own investigation, go right ahead."

I nodded at the bag of evidence. "Anything good come off the inhaler?"

She shook her head. "It belongs to a kid named Scott Turner. We checked with the resort. He and his mother stayed here the same week you and Benji did. Just a coincidence."

"Scott Turner," I murmured. "Why does that name sound familiar?"

"Probably because you want it to," Mila said. "Look, I'm tired. You want to get a drink? For old time's sake? Give me an hour of peace, then I'll let you pick my brain about the case."

"Deal."

ALL THIS TIME, I'd been hoping Petra was downplaying the amount of information they had on Benji's disappearance. According to Mila, she hadn't. Benji had disappeared without a trace. Other than the missing maid and his weird drawing, they had nothing to base their investigation on. From the look on Mila's face, I could tell she was long past worry and into self-hatred.

After midnight, I left her in the cigar bar and headed upstairs to the new room I'd checked into, determined to get a good night's sleep and start fresh tomorrow. Mila might have given up hope, but I sure hadn't. I refused to accept that I'd never see Benji again.

I swiped my hotel key and stepped inside. As soon as I did, something on the floor caught my eye. Someone had shoved a sheet of paper under the door. I picked it up. The letter-writer had glued cut-out magazine letters to a piece of Wolf Park Ski Resort stationary. As I read the mismatched writing, my jaw dropped.

Get Benji back. Drop 500k at 3 Saint John Drive. You have three days. No cops or he dies.

12

My first instinct was to run back to the cigar bar and show the creepy cut-and-paste ransom letter to Mila, but the last few words on the page instilled fear in the deepest part of my soul.

No cops or he dies.

Ransoms were tricky. When kids were involved, it was safest to hand over the money. Hell, entire police departments paid hackers to get access to their stolen databases back. There was only one problem: I didn't have half a million dollars to hand over to whatever sicko had stolen Benji.

"Who are you?" I muttered, tracing the mismatched letters.

Another fact about ransoms popped into my mind; the victim was intentionally targeted. In my case, that didn't make sense. Anyone in my life knew I didn't have anywhere close to five hundred thousand dollars in the bank, so who would kidnap Benji and demand that much? Obviously, this person didn't know me well enough to be privy to my current financial situation.

3 Saint John Drive.

I logged on to my laptop and typed in the address. On the map, I zoomed it on the street view. The address belonged to a cute house in a nearby neighborhood, not twenty minutes from the ski resort. A quick search told me that, like the rest of Wolf Park, it was a low-crime area. People tended to leave their cars and doors unlocked.

It wasn't the usual spot to drop off a ransom payment. Generally, the kidnapper demanded you jump through a few hoops to get the money to a safe spot. I'd done all sorts of crazy crap in the past, including dumping five thousand dollars in cash down a sewer drain in an airtight Tupperware container for the culprit to find downstream. Of course, we had a team of special agents stationed along the sewer route, so when the kidnapper did get the money, he also got arrested.

This time was different. I didn't have the same resources now that I wasn't officially working with the agency. I had to figure this out on my own. Without the money, that meant I had one solid option: stake out in front of the address before the drop-off date to catch the kidnapper in action.

No cops or he dies.

The phrase echoed through my head, repeated by a demonic, bodiless voice that my imagination created. I lay in bed, fully clothed, and let the effects of tonight's whiskey wash over me, wishing I had more to lure me to sleep. My thoughts tumbled and rushed over one another like river rapids. Without a lifeline to pull me to shore, I would drown in the terrible possibilities that awaited Benji.

I dragged my suitcase out from under the bed and sifted through it until I found my bathroom bag. Toothpaste, face wash, deodorant… but no anti-anxiety medications. Shit. Had I left the bottle at home in my rush to get out of the house?

I texted Ophelia.

Hey, O. Can you check my bathroom for a bottle labeled Fluoxetine?

The reply came within a minute: *Yup. In your medicine cabinet. What's it for?*

I smacked my forehead. "Stupid, stupid, stupid."

Don't worry about it. Thanks for checking.

Ophelia's know-it-all tone was evident in her answer. *I have Google. I can look it up.*

It's for anxiety, okay? I wrote back. *I didn't want you kids to know.*

If Ophelia was judging me, she didn't bother to

let me know. *Do you need me to ship it to you? I can go to the post office tomorrow.*

It's illegal to mail prescriptions, I replied. *I'll figure something out.*

My phone was quiet for a few minutes, and I figured Ophelia was finished talking to me. Her limited attention span didn't last too long, especially during a conversation with her mother.

My mind drifted back to Benji and his captor. The culprit obviously had it out for me, but as I wracked my brain, I couldn't recall anyone who'd sworn revenge on me. I didn't exactly lead a life of rebellion and vengeance. The only person who had a grudge about me was Pam from the high school PTA, all because Ophelia had once been chosen for a part in a play over Pam's daughter Emma. Ophelia never learned the lines, ruined the performance, and admitted she'd only tried out to screw over Emma. If Pam were guilty, she most likely would have kidnapped Ophelia. Not Benji.

I rubbed my eyes. Clearly, the whiskey had kicked in. No one in the PTA was ballsy enough to steal one of my children and demand five hundred thousand for his safe return. That meant someone else had a problem with me. Or what if this was all Amos's fault?

"Go to sleep, Carolina," I ordered myself.

I took a leaf out of Ophelia's book and covered

my face with a pillow to block out the happy sounds of people partying outside. My cheap room was on the second floor of the resort, which meant I could hear every damn conversation from the bars, restaurants, and streets below. The pillow stifled the voices and shouts, but my head throbbed from too much alcohol and not enough water. Not to mention, drinking wasn't recommended while taking anti-anxiety medication. The counter-indications weren't pretty.

Despite the worry eating away at my soul, I eventually found sleep. Unfortunately, it wasn't as restful as I hoped.

"WHAT DO WE GOT?"

My voice, sharp and authoritative, rang through the office. The other agents on my team scrambled to answer the question.

"Got a location, ma'am," said Brooks, a short guy with a goatee who was a whiz with computer stuff. He was one of the reasons we'd gotten so far on this case in such a short amount of time. "Corner of Green and Twelfth Street."

"Let's move out," I ordered.

The scene changed without warning. Cramped in a surveillance truck with Mila, Brooks, and a few other agents, we crowded around the screens and watched the action outside unfold.

The ugly street corner featured a crappy apartment building. Judging by the residents we'd seen going in and out, at least one person was cooking meth in that basement. Not the safest place to live, let alone hold a kidnapped child. Our culprit was in for a shock.

I brought a radio to my lips. "Can we confirm the child's location?"

On the video, I watched one of my agents shift through the bushes along the side of the apartment building. He was so well camouflaged that no one else noticed he was there. He peeked through the side window, into the apartment we'd flagged earlier.

"Got eyes on the kid," he muttered quietly into his microphone. "Perp not in sight though. Hold for confirmation."

Another one of my guys, who we called Boomer, loitered on the street corner, dressed in a stained sweatshirt, ugly jeans, and a ratty hoody. If I didn't know who he was, I would have mistaken him for another junkie stopping by the apartment building in the hope of finding a quick fix.

Boomer kept an eye on the back door of the building. He lifted his wrist to his mouth and wiped his nose, but a microphone was hidden beneath his sleeve. "Perp's car just pulled up around the corner. Waiting for visual... Got it. He's heading inside."

A moment later, my agent in the bushes radioed in. "Got eyes on the kid and the perp. Ready to enter."

"Go, go, go!" I ordered.

My team sprang into action. They leapt out of bushes, concealed cars, and other hiding places. The kevlar vests beneath their clothes made them look more bulky and muscular than they were in real life. I watched as they covered all the exits of the building then kicked the door in.

Triumph burst like fireworks in my chest when my guys appeared on the front walk, carrying the perp between them. The man guilty of kidnapping his own four-year-old child looked like he hadn't seen the sun or a barber in years. Scraggly gray-brown hair hung in matted clumps around his shoulders. The shape of his face was lost in an ugly beard. He wore a white tank top with questionable yellow and red stains on it and no jacket, despite the chill outside.

My lip curled as the man kicked and screamed, trying to dislodge himself from my agents' grip.

"That's my son!" he hollered. "Don't take my son."

"You don't have custody, bastard," I muttered under my breath, even though the perp couldn't hear me from inside the surveillance van. "And the kid doesn't deserve to live in a dump."

Once the perp was out of sight, my guys came out with the kid. I glanced at the footage, trying to determine if the young boy was hurt and needed medical attention.

The dream warped. The boy's face changed.
It was Benji.

I WOKE UP, gasping for air like a fish on a hook. The sheets were soaked with sweat. I rolled out of them, went to the bathroom, and flipped up the toilet seat. I hovered over it, waiting for my stomach to decide what it wanted to do. Thankfully, the urge to heave settled. I sat on the edge of the bathtub to catch my breath.

That case, the one from my dream, was the first one I'd ever run point on. Mila was a newbie, just recruited to the agency, and I was determined to prove myself in a position of leadership. The four-year-old boy, whose name I'd forgotten, was perfectly okay when we finally found and extracted him from the situation. Later, when we sent the police in to investigate the apartment building, we learned that the basement was indeed used for making meth. The whole place was a few batches away from blowing up.

Benji hadn't even been born them. My paranoid self inserted him in that scenario. Then again, he could be in more danger than I anticipated.

I took a cold shower to wash off the salty sweat and anxiety that stuck to my skin. After getting dressed, I pocketed the ransom letter and went downstairs to the lobby. A week ago, I was just like all these other moms, tugging their children along to go skiing and snowboarding, with no worries other than forcing my family to have fun. Now, as they passed me by, I envied every tiny detail of their lives. I mentally screenshot each bright smile a small child exchanged with their mother or father. I let my gaze trail after boys with Benji's height and stature, wishing my son would magically reappear.

I skipped breakfast, unsure of what my stomach could handle, and opted for a single cup of matcha green tea. Bracing myself against the cold, I jogged across the parking lot and got into my car. As the heater warmed up, I plugged in the address of the drop-off site for the ransom payment. Eighteen minutes away. It couldn't be this simple.

On the road, my Bluetooth connection trilled. *"Call from Ophelia."*

I pushed to answer. "O? Aren't you supposed to be in school?"

"Yeah, I'm in the bathroom during passing period," she said. "You never answered my text last night."

"I didn't get another text from you."

"Yes, you did. Check your phone."

At a red light, I flipped to the unread messages on my phone. Last night, after I'd fallen asleep in a whiskey daze, Ophelia had asked, *Are you going to be okay?*

"Oh, honey," I said, focusing on the road again as the light turned green. "I don't want you to worry about me. I'll be fine."

"But I looked up those pills," she said. "You're not supposed to stop taking them without a doctor's permission. You could have side effects or withdrawal issues. You should call your doctor and ask them to fill the prescription somewhere in Wolf Park."

"I'll handle it, O. Thanks for looking out for me." I heard the bell ring over the phone. "Go to class, honey. You're going to be late."

She cleared her throat. "Mom, please come home safely. I can't lose you too."

"You won't, O. I promise."

"Okay. Gotta go."

"Love you, baby." Jokingly, I added, "Make good choices."

"I always do," she said seriously before hanging up.

FIVE MINUTES LATER, I turned into a nice neighborhood with perfectly-trimmed hedges, matching mailboxes, and a collection of petite dogs walked by equally petite owners. No one in this area had left up their Christmas lights past New Year's. Doing so would easily put you in the riffraff category.

At first, I cruised by 3 Saint John Drive at a snail's pace, just to check the place out. It matched the street view picture on Google Maps. Nice red brick accents, pretty white shutters, and real poinsettias framing the front porch. It looked nothing like the apartment building ready to explode from the meth basement. Reasonably, a child would be safe inside this house.

I kept driving, lest someone noticed me lingering on their safe neighborhood street and report me to whatever inane police officer watched over this portion of Wolf Park. Thankfully, a row of high holly bushes served as a perfect place to hide my car and stake out, just around the corner from the cute little house with the white shutters.

I got comfortable, pushing my seat away from the steering wheel and perching my feet on the dashboard. I found a podcast about baking and played it over the car speakers. As I nursed my matcha latte, I kept a keen eye on 3 Saint John Drive. If anyone came or went, I would see them.

Stakeouts, by nature, were incredibly boring. Back in the day, with Mila by my side, the time passed more quickly. We kept ourselves entertained by swapping gossip, philosophical dilemmas, and stories about our kids. With a heavy stash of protein bars, crackers, cookies, and water, we could snack and gab for hours. Any time outside the FBI offices had to be cherished, even if it meant staring at the door to a crack shack for hours at a time while we waited for our suspect to arrive.

Alone, things were different. The baking podcast was boring, mostly because I didn't have much interest in baking. The only reason I'd chosen to listen to it was so I could make those biscuits for Ophelia and Benji when we were all together again. The woman on the podcast didn't talk about biscuits, though. Her talk about yeast, proving times, and metric system measurements blended together into a haze of nonsense. I had no idea what she was trying to explain, but at least now I knew how to pronounce *croquembouche* correctly.

The other perk to having a partner during a stakeout was having someone to keep you awake, focused, and alert. More than once, my gaze strayed from the house as yet another housewife strolled along the sidewalk with a purse-sized dog. After a while, the caffeine from my green tea gave up. Each time I nodded off, I accidentally bumped my forehead against the window, which jolted me awake again.

To make matters worse, an uncomfortable heat grew in my lower abdomen. Recalling my conversation with Ophelia, I searched for "symptoms of withdrawal" for my medication and immediately found "digestive upset" on the list.

"Great," I muttered as my intestines gurgled. "Guess I'm going to have to speed this process up a bit."

Against my better judgement, I got out of the car. With a ball cap drawn low over my face, I approached the house on Saint John Drive. Thankfully, no housewives were around to witness as I crept through the front yard and hopped the privacy fence. Once out of the public view, I cupped my hands against the nearest window and peered inside.

The kitchen was empty, and as I worked my way around the first floor, the rest of the rooms proved silent as well. With clenched teeth, I gripped the back door handle and turned it. It clicked open. Whoever lived here trusted their neighbors enough not to rob them.

It smelled like yeast inside, like someone had baked fresh bread that morning, but it didn't cover the stuffy musk of the antique furniture. If I had to guess, the people who lived here were quite old. The TV was still hooked up to a cable box, and a locked cabinet full of porcelain dishes decorated the far wall of the living room.

A set of photos above the mantel confirmed my suspicions. Each one featured the same man and woman throughout several years of their marriage.

By the look of the latest one, the couple was in their late sixties or early seventies. In most of the photos, they were accompanied by a boy around Ophelia's age, who must have been their grandson. If their wide smiles were any indication, both Grandma and Grandpa were proud of the teenager between them.

My intestines gurgled again as I made my way through the house. I swallowed my discomfort and kept going, careful not to touch anything. Doubt crept into my head as I realized there was nothing here to connect the elderly people who owned this place to Benji. They weren't exactly prime suspects.

A pile of mail sat on a table near the front door. I peeked at the address labels. *Copper and Glinda Billings.* Even their names were old. I took a picture of the topmost envelope with my phone so I could look the couple up later. As I did so, Mila's name and number popped up on the screen.

"Where are you?" Mila asked when I answered.

"Uh—" I couldn't exactly admit I'd broken into someone's home.

"Whatever, just get back to the resort," she said. "I found something."

"Sure." My stomach lurched. "As soon as I go to the bathroom."

13

After stopping at the nearest gas station to relieve myself, my stomach situation somewhat improved. I was nowhere near feeling normal, though. I bought a liter of water and chugged it on the way back to the resort. Not long after, my skin broke out in a cold sweat that smelled none too pleasant. These side effects were no joke, or maybe the stress of everything was finally getting to me.

Mila met me in the parking lot, her arms crossed. As I stumbled out of the car, she raised an eyebrow. "Are you drunk?"

"No," I said, working to regain my balance. "But dear God, I wish I was."

Mila steadied me and let me lean on her. "What the hell is wrong with you?"

"I left my meds at home."

"Shit. That's an issue. Let's get you inside. Petra's waiting."

"Petra?" Just the sound of the detective's name made me want to hurl. "What, are you and her like best friends now?"

Mila dragged me up the front walk of the resort. Mothers shielded their children from me as we passed. Did I really look that terrible?

"We need each other," Mila said. "Where have you been anyway? Hopefully not snooping around anywhere else."

"In that case, it's probably best if I keep my recent whereabouts to myself then."

Mila sighed. "Do you know how many strings I had to pull to keep you from getting arrested yesterday?"

"Quite a few, I imagine." I let out a foul burp. "Oh, God. I feel like someone tossed my organs into a blender."

Mila leaned out of my gas cloud. "Thank you for that lovely image. Can you make it through this meeting or what?"

"I need Pepto-Bismol and a very large glass of ginger ale. Real ginger ale. Not soda. The cigar bar can make it."

She hauled me through the lobby. "They make it?"

"Mm-hmm. With fresh ginger. Settles the stomach. Please—" I made grabby hands at the archway that led to the bar. "I won't be any use if I feel this nasty."

"You were never like this at the agency," Mila grumbled, changing her path to include the bar.

"That was before I ever felt the soul-crushing agony of losing a child," I reminded her. "A mother shuts down after trauma like that."

"You haven't lost Benji," Mila snapped. "Not yet anyway. And if you pull yourself together long enough to hear what me and Petra found out, we might have a shot at getting him back."

"Where is the precious Detective Lee anyway?"

"In my room."

"Kinky. I didn't know you swung that way. That's cool," I prattled on, half out of my mind. "I think Ophelia's gay. She hates boys, but that could be a teenaged girl thing, right? Do you think she'll tell me or do I have to pry it out of her?"

"I think, if that is the case, you should probably let your daughter come out at her own pace," Mila replied reasonably. "Don't pressure her. Are you sure you're not drunk?"

"I feel worse than drunk."

She deposited me on a stool and flagged the bartender. "Fresh ginger ale for this woman, please. Carolina, drink. Take an ibuprofen. I'm going to see what I can do about this medication issue. Give me a minute."

She drifted off to a private corner to make a call. The bartender set the ale in front of me with a fresh slice of ginger floating on top.

"Sure you don't want something stronger?" he asked with a wink. "Hair of the dog?"

"God, no. Please go away. I'll give you a huge tip if you don't talk to me."

Unsure whether or not to be offended, he left to serve another customer. I hunkered over my drink and chewed on the ginger. The fresh spiciness cut through my cloud of brain fog, helping to clear my head. As it made its way through my digestive tract, my stomach began to settle. I scrolled through results of my "what to do when you accidentally skip your anti-anxiety meds" search on my phone until Mila returned.

"Good news," she said. "I called in yet another favor on your behalf. You'll be able to pick up a week's worth supply of your meds at the local pharmacy tomorrow morning. You're welcome." She studied me as I slumped over the counter. "Seriously, Carolina. I've never seen you like this before, not even when things turned upside down with Amos. You usually keep a level head."

To my utter embarrassment, my eyes filled with tears. As fat globs of saltwater rolled over my cheeks,

Mila awkwardly looked in the other direction. I furiously wiped my eyes.

"Damn, I never cry in front of coworkers," I said.

"Good thing we're not coworkers anymore," Mila replied. She weaved her arm underneath mine and lifted me from the stool. "We're friends, remember? We deal with each other, even at our worst. Come on. Let's get you upstairs."

Mila's suite was twice the size of the room I'd rented for my family last week, complete with a miniature kitchen, a separate bedroom, and a bathroom that included a Jacuzzi tub.

"Wow, the agency went all out for you, huh?" I asked. "I never got digs like this."

Petra emerged from the bathroom, patting her hands dry with a fresh towel. For once, she wasn't wearing a pantsuit.

"Jeans?" I questioned. "Who the hell are you?"

"Hello, Carolina," she said, ignoring my demand. "It's nice to see you again." Her nose wrinkled as she stepped closer to me. "Not so nice to smell you, though. What on earth is that stench?"

"It's her," Mila confirmed.

I backed away from both of them. "Is it really that bad?"

Petra plugged her nose. "It's like rotting broccoli."

"But more subtle," Mila added, trying to comfort me.

"It's coming out of my pores," I whispered.

With two fingers, Petra piloted me to the sofa and cracked the window behind it. "Just sit there…" She retreated to the kitchenette table, next to Mila. "And we'll sit over here."

I pulled my hair up so the cool air from outside washed across the back of my neck and dried the sweat there. I wished I could afford my armpits the same treatment, but I decided to spare Mila and Petra that horrible experience.

"Well?" I prompted. "You dragged me up here. What did you find?"

"Remember the fake maid?" Mila asked.

"The one who broke into my room and disappeared from your custody?" I said. "Yeah, I remember her. What about it?"

"We finally got her real name," Petra said. "Aubrey Wharton. Nomadic ne'er-do-well."

I waited for more, but neither woman added any details. "That's it? So what?"

Mila braved my stench to cross the room and hand me a file. "We're in the process of tracking her down. We think she's still in the area."

I flipped through the Aubrey Wharton's paperwork. She was a small-time criminal. Petty theft, drug dealing, and a little bit of sex work on the side.

"Not exactly the kind of woman you'd want babysitting your kids. How'd she end up in Wolf Park to begin with?"

"We don't care how she got here," Petra said. "We're more interested in why she posed as a maid and broke into your room."

"Someone hired her," I suggested.

"What makes you think she's not the perp?" Petra asked.

I lifted one of Aubrey Wharton's mug shots. "This is not the face of a kidnapper. She's just trying to keep herself alive. My bet is she had a shitty childhood with shitty parents. Never had anyone to take care of her, and this is the kind of crap she has to do for a little cash."

"Women like that also work for human trafficking cartels," Petra reminded me. "Easier to lure victims as a friendly lady."

"If she worked for a cartel, they wouldn't have bothered with Benji's insulin," I said. "Cartels want kids who can sustain a lot of trauma, not ones reliant on medication. No, the kidnapper wants to keep him alive."

"But why?" Mila asked. "What do they want? Money?" Her eyebrows went up. "Carolina, did you get a ransom letter?"

My heart rate tripled. The cut-and-pasted note

burned white hot against the inside pocket of my pants. "No."

Mila's shoulders slumped. "Damn. None of this is making sense. We need to get this Wharton girl back in for questioning."

"Any idea where she is?" I asked. "You said she was still in the area."

The investigators exchanged an annoyed glance.

"One of my officers picked her up for stealing at a convenience store near the county line," Petra said.

"Great." I closed the file. "Where are you holding her?"

Petra cleared her throat. "I didn't say we had her."

"What do you mean?"

"The officer let her go," Mila answered. "He didn't know we put out a BOLO out for her."

I gaped at them. "He didn't *know?*"

"He was looking for Ella Smart," Petra said defensively. "Not Aubrey Wharton."

"Isn't her picture on the BOLO?"

Petra simpered. "Regardless, we don't have her."

"But we'll find her again," Mila assured me. "Now that we have her real name."

I rose from the couch and ambled toward the door.

"Where are you going?" the investigators asked at the same time.

"I'm going to take a nap," I declared. "And when I

wake up, I expect the two of you to have good news for me. Got it?"

I didn't wait for an answer and let myself out of Mila's room. As the door drifted shut, I heard her say to Petra, "*That's* what she was like at the agency. No nonsense and no patience."

IN MY OWN ROOM, I ran a warm bath, added as many bubbles as the tub could hold, and sank in up to my nose. The water ran into my ears, filling my head with white noise. I closed my eyes and savored the relative peace of the resort bathroom. If only I could suspend my existence and stay here for a while, then nothing else would matter as much.

Alas, that was not the way the world worked. Despite Mila's excitement, she and Petra had hardly made any progress. Sure, getting the fake maid's real name was a step forward, but they wouldn't earn any gold stars for that.

I reached over the edge of the tub, dried my hands on a nearby towel, and pulled the ransom letter from my pants pocket. As I unfolded it and studied the menacing threat once more, I tried to look at it from an investigator's point of view rather than a mother's.

The cut-out R gave it away. It so obviously belonged to a *Rolling Stone* cover, as did a few other letters pasted to the page. I studied the various fonts, wondering if I could pinpoint what other magazines the kidnapper had used to put the letter together.

The challenge drew me out of the tub before I had the chance to truly relax. Dripping water across the floor, I wrapped a towel around myself and sat at the desk. On my laptop, I navigated to the Wolf Park Ski Resort's Wi-Fi connection page. As soon as the connection was established, the page refreshed, offering additional accommodations like room service, newspaper delivery, and pay per view for a fee. I clicked on the list of magazines available for delivery. Using the ransom letter as a guide, I scrolled through the cover pictures and compared them side by side with the letter.

After a solid hour, I determined the ransom letter had been compiled from four different magazines: *Rolling Stone*, *People*, *Snowboarder*, and *Method*. The latter two served the snowboarding population at Wolf Park, which meant whoever had pasted together the letter had some sort of interest in the sport. I called the front desk.

"Wolf Park Ski Resort front desk," a cheerful voice said. "What can I help you with?"

"This is Special Agent Mila Dulik with the FBI," I said in my best impression of my friend. "I need a favor. Can you look something up for me?"

"Sure thing, Agent Dulik."

"I need the room numbers and names of anyone who has ordered these four magazines in the last two weeks." I recited the magazine names over the phone. "Have any guests received all four titles at once?"

"Let me see," the receptionist muttered. "That's an odd combo, so it shouldn't be too many. Ah, here we go. Yes, one guest requested those four titles in Cabin Six. If you head into our resort village, Cabin Six is the third one on the right-hand side. Do you need anything else?"

"That'll be all. Thanks for your help."

I hung up, feeling triumphant. It was the barest hint of a lead, but it was a lead nonetheless. I dried my hair and got dressed.

Wrapped up in my ski coat and boots, I strolled toward the resort village. Long ago, I'd been more familiar with this area than the rest of the resort, but all the renovations made things look different. Cabin Six was once a cozy one-story log-built house. Now, the first ten cabins along the pathway were two stories high and could accommodate at least ten people each.

I walked up the cobblestone pathway to the front of Cabin Six and lifted my hand to knock on the door. Before my knuckles landed, a teenaged boy with long blond hair and expensive designer sunglasses emerged from inside, nearly knocking me over as he carried his snowboard over the threshold.

"Whoa, sorry!" he said, leaning his snowboard against the cabin to help me up. "Didn't expect anyone to be waiting outside here. Are you Tim's girlfriend? He said he was dating an older woman, but you're, like, way older."

I quickly let go of the teenager's arm once I got my footing. "No, I am not Tim's girlfriend. My name is Special Agent Mila Dulik. I'm with the FBI."

He laughed outright. "You're shitting me."

I squared my shoulders. "I am not. Do you have a minute? I have some questions for you and anyone else staying at this cabin."

"That might be a problem," the boy said. "Everyone else is on the slopes, except for my mom, who's probably at the bar. What's this about?"

I took the ransom note out of my pocket and let him look at it. "You ever seen this before?"

"No, ma'am. Kinda creepy, though."

"These letters came from four different magazines," I informed him, "all of which were delivered to this cabin within the last week."

The teenager's eyebrows lifted. "So you think one of my friends sent this letter?"

"That's what I'm trying to figure out."

"Ma'am," he said, exasperated. "No offense, but I

think you're after the wrong information. Everyone staying here is around my age, minus my mom. None of them have a reason to write a letter like that. We're at Wolf Park for a snowboarding competition."

"What about the magazines?" I asked. "Can I see them?"

"Sure. Wait here. I'll see if I can find them."

As the kid went inside to look, I stomped my feet to warm them up and watched my breath float away on the wind. A few minutes later, the teenager returned.

"So this is weird," he said. "But I can only find one, and—well, see for yourself."

He handed over a tattered magazine. The cover had been completely torn off, along with several pages throughout the middle.

"Has anyone else been here?" I asked. "People other than your friends?"

The teenager guiltily scratched his head. "We had a party a few nights ago when my mom was out. A bunch of people showed up."

"Can I get their names?"

"If I knew them, I'd give them to you," the teenager said. "But I have no idea who those people were."

"You invited random people to party with you?"

He shrugged. "We left the door open. Anyone could have come in."

I kneaded my temples. "Is there any way I could track down who might have done this to the magazine?"

"There's another party tonight."

"I don't think—"

"We're professionals," the teenager interrupted. "Me and my friends are professional snowboarders. Not to sound like a jackass, but we run in tight packs. The snowboarding scene stays the same in every city. One party in Wolf Park attracts the same people as another party in Wolf Park."

I picked up his point. "So you're saying if I crash this party tonight, I might run into the person who made this letter?"

The teenager nodded. "But don't go in there looking like a narc. No one will talk to you if they think you're gonna bust them for weed."

"Duly noted."

14

Naturally, the snowboarders' house party didn't start until well after eleven o'clock. The address the blond teenager had given me led me to a neighborhood full of huge houses, north of the ski resort. The fancy community, with its security checkpoints and recreation center, reeked with privilege. I wrinkled my nose as I tailed another car through the automatic gates at the front of the neighborhood. The people who could afford to live in a place like this were lucky suckers.

The house in question seemed to be one of the biggest on the block. It rose a good four stories, and looked twice as wide as it was tall. Around the side, I spotted a pool house and a separate garage. Expensive cars lined the large circular driveway. My eight-year-old minivan paled in comparison. As guests began to arrive, either by Uber or from other pricey vehicles, I parked down the street and watched.

Nondescript house music pumped through the street, loudly enough for a few neighbors to come out to see what was going on. After shaking their heads, they retreated to their own homes. No cops showed up, so parties of this magnitude must have been pretty commonplace here.

From what I could tell, all the guests were between the ages of fourteen and twenty. A truck delivered several kegs, though, so someone had to be legal enough to buy drinks inside. I hoped a set of irresponsible parents weren't dumb enough to buy their kids that much beer. Considering the amount of people showing up to the party, I had a feeling the owner of the house had no idea what was happening here.

More and more teenagers poured in, until it was impossible to drive by without noticing the party inside. The windows shone with multi-colored lights and silhouettes of gyrating bodies. Boys and girls spilled out of the house and onto the front porch and yard, wildly throwing snowballs at each other without coats. Someone started a bonfire with a bunch of pizza boxes and a lighter. All in all, it looked like the perfect place for a tragic teenaged death to occur.

"Don't dress like a narc," I muttered, repeating

the advice given to me earlier that afternoon as I tugged at the front of my jeans to smooth out the wrinkles. "What the hell does that mean?"

In this crowd, my age would stand out like a sore thumb. I had to fly under the radar somehow. I glanced over my shoulder, looking for something else I could use to get inside. Ophelia's favorite sweatshirt—a black hoodie with an ugly band logo printed on the back—lay across the seat. It smelled like stale potato chips and soda. I pulled it on. The sleeves were much too short, but the oversized hood obscured most of my face. With any luck, no one would notice the middle-aged mom in the midst of their teenaged depravity.

I got out of the car, braced myself for what awaited me inside, and crossed the street to the party house. A young girl, no older than Ophelia, was already throwing up in the bushes. No one bothered to hold her hair, so it swung freely into the mess. I grimaced and looked away. Every instinct screamed for me to help her—who knew how much alcohol she had already consumed—but I couldn't give myself away. With any luck, one of her friends would take care of her.

"In and out," I told myself. "Get the information you need. Then call the cops and shut this shit down."

When I walked inside, I automatically wished for

Petra to show up. The place was a disaster. Empty cups, trash, and used paper plates littered the floor. Teenagers walked over shattered ceramic from a broken vase without noticing the danger. One boy didn't have shoes on. I grabbed his arm and navigated him away from the glass. He saluted me and strolled straight into a wall.

Bass pounded in my head as I moved into the first living room. It was packed with bodies, girls and boys grinding their hips together. Some of them moved awkwardly, like this was the first time they'd ever danced with the opposite sex. Others knew too well what they were doing and what it could lead to.

In one corner, a few people bowed their heads over a reflective table. I spied the line of drugs before someone sucked the powder up their nose with a rolled-up dollar bill. In another corner, half-hidden behind a decorative palm tree, a pair of sixteen-year-olds hooked up without a care in the world that the whole party could see them.

A haze of smoke hung above the crowd. Half the kids had vape pens. They drew long breaths from their devices and released enormous clouds of white vapor into the air. The acrid smell of marijuana mingled with the fruity flavored juice emanating from the vapes. I resisted the urge to plug my nose as I forced my way across the room.

I had no idea where to start. There were at least a

hundred people here, and I doubted a single one was sober enough to answer my questions about the ransom letter. Perhaps this was all a big mistake. I took out my phone, ready to call Mila and Petra, so they could shut down the party.

A hand fell on my shoulder.

"Hey, you made it!"

I turned around to find the blond teenager from earlier that day. His eyes were bloodshot, but he wore a wide smile. He took his hand from my shoulder and held it out to me instead.

"Charlie!" he shouted over the thumping music. He held up a lit joint. "Want some of this?"

I shook my head. "Do you recognize anyone from your last party? Who should I talk to?"

Charlie took a long drag from the joint, and I feared for the dying cells in his young developing brain. He pointed across the room, toward the group inhaling cocaine in the corner.

"Those guys were definitely there," he yelled. "But I didn't let them bring that shit into my cabin. I'm strictly an herbal guy."

"I don't care about your drug use," I hollered back. "Though you shouldn't smoke too much until you turn twenty-five. Your brain—"

He burst out laughing and cradled his stomach. "You're the coolest FBI agent I've ever met, lady. You should come to my school and do a career talk. I'm home-schooled though, so you'd just be coming to my house." A look of confusion crossed his face. "Isn't it weird how home and school are the same place sometimes? It's like—I go to school, but I'm still home. Right?" He dissolved into laughter again. "Wild!"

I grit my teeth. Clearly, Charlie was too stoned to be of much use to me. "Does your mom know you're here?"

"Technically, yes."

I nodded toward the joint. "Does she know what you're doing?"

"Eh." He waved his hand in a so-so gesture. "Don't worry about it. Hey, look! That guy was totally at my party. You could talk to him. Or find Toto. He knows everything."

I followed the direction of Charlie's finger across the room, but pinpointing one person at the end of it was impossible. "Which guy? Who's Toto? Charlie, I—"

But the teenager had disappeared. Rage prickled across the back of my neck as I studied the faces in the room, trying to guess who might have been at the resort the night the ransom letter was crafted. My gaze slid across a woman's face—she seemed familiar. I looked back at her and gasped.

It was the fake maid: Aubrey Wharton.

Like me, she was one of the older people in the

room, though she had a better shot at blending in since she was just shy of twenty-five. Also like me, she seemed to be steering clear of any drugs or alcohol. Her eyes were clear as she shook a tall teenaged boy by the shoulder and shouted something in his ear. He rolled his eyes and pointed in the opposite direction.

I cut swiftly through the crowd before I realized I looked like a shark hunting in bloody waters. Quickly, I fell into the shadows and watched as Aubrey Wharton made her way across the party. Her face fell into a glum expression as she fished a bottle of water out of a big cooler. As she shook the ice off her hand, I stepped into her path.

"Aubrey Wharton?" I asked.

She fixed me with a hard stare. "Yeah, what's it to you?"

I seized her by the upper arm and yanked her toward the first door in my eye line. She pulled and yelled, resisting as much as possible, but I'd perfected my vise grip long ago. No one paid attention to her pleas for help. They were all too drunk or high.

I kicked open the door and found a spare bedroom. Of course, it was occupied by two teenagers with their pants around their ankles.

"Out!" I barked.

They yanked their clothes on and sheepishly slid

out of the room. I tossed Aubrey Wharton inside and locked the door behind me.

She rubbed the red welt on her arm from where my fingers had locked tightly around her skin. "Who the hell do you think you are? I could have you arrested for assault!"

"My name is Carolina Caccia," I said in a deadly whisper. "You broke into my room at the Wolf Park Ski Resort about a week ago, posing as a maid."

The color drained from Aubrey's face. She held her hands in a defensive position. "Look, lady. I don't know anything about that. Someone hired me—"

I slammed my fist against the wall, making her jump.

"Who?" I demanded. "Who hired you?"

"I don't know his name!" she answered frantically. "Hell, I never even saw his face. I talked to the kid."

My heart stopped and my head roared. "The kid? What kid?"

"When I went to meet the guy to get the instructions for the job, a kid met me instead," she said, calmer now that she could see my interest in the subject. "He was probably seven or eight years old. About yea high." She hovered her hand about four feet above the ground. "He seemed scared to death."

"Where did you meet him?"

"At the corner shop near the resort."

"Was he safe? Did he look hurt?"

"He looked fine," she reported, shrugging. "Just scared. Shaking a little."

I dropped my head into my hands. This woman had seen Benji after he'd been taken. He was okay. Or at least, he had been on the day she'd broken into our room.

"That was my son," I said in a cracked voice. "He was kidnapped, and someone is holding him for ransom."

Aubrey's mouth dropped open. "Oh my God, I am so sorry. If I'd known—" The sentence trailed off. "Look, for what it's worth, I did what he asked me to do without taking his money."

Confusion clouded my head. "Wait, my son hired you?"

"I assume so," she replied. "He gave me a room key he'd picked off someone else. Then he told me to get his insulin from the fridge and leave a creepy drawing on the floor somewhere. He told me *you* would find it."

I sat on the edge of the bed. Aubrey sidled around me, heading for the door, but I caught her by the skirt. "Don't go anywhere yet. I have more questions. Why didn't you call the police?"

She guilty chewed her lip. "To be honest, I needed the money. He offered me fifty bucks. Then when I got there and I realized who hired me, I figured the kid needed the money *and* his medicine more than I needed fifty dollars. I don't ask questions about the jobs I take. I do them, get paid, and move on with my life. I'm sorry you and your son got caught in the crossfire." Her eyes widened, as if recalling new information. "Oh my God. I can totally help you."

"What are you talking about?" I muttered.

"I just talked to Toto—"

"That's the second time I've heard that name," I said. "Who the hell is Toto?"

"He's a dealer," Aubrey answered nonchalantly. "Actually, he's a supplier, but he deals too. How do you think these kids got ahold of all those drugs? He's smart. Knows how to sell to young people because he's young himself."

"What does he have to do with my son?"

Aubrey rubbed her hands together like a hungry fly. "The thing about Toto is he doesn't just deal recreational drugs. He can get prescriptions as well. Like insulin."

"I'm listening."

"I asked him to hook me up with some weed to sell," Aubrey went on. "But he was complaining that he had too many jobs to do. Some dude asked him to get insulin cartridges for a kid's pump. I thought it was weird that we both did a run for the same medication, so I asked him about it."

I leaned forward, my pulse racing. "What did he say?"

"At that point, some idiot came up asking Toto for coke, so I didn't get the full story," Aubrey said. "But you should find Toto. He hangs out at all of these dumb parties for the snowboarders, and he knows Wolf Park like the back of his hand. He's your best bet." Tentatively, she got up to leave. "Are you going to grab me again?"

Wearily, I shook my head. "I got what I needed out of you. You should know, though. The police and the FBI are looking for you in conjunction with my son's case. It's in your best interest to get out of the state."

She nodded. "Thanks for the heads-up."

Once she slipped out, I allowed myself ninety seconds to lay on the bed and absorb all the information Aubrey had given me. Number one: she'd seen Benji alive and well. Number two: Benji had enough freedom to get ahold of his insulin and leave me a message, but why hadn't he used that freedom to call the police? Number three: this guy Toto might have all the answers I needed.

I rolled off the bed, took a deep breath, and dove back into the party. Each time I spotted a teenager who looked in better control of his or her faculties, I pulled them aside.

"Have you seen Toto?"

"Nope."

"Hey, do you know where Toto is?"

"Sorry, lady."

"Is Toto—?"

"Get off me, narc."

The last girl shook free of me and shot me a furtive look as she disappeared into the crowd. I let out a long sigh. This was harder than I thought it would be.

I glanced toward the far corner of the living room again, where a different group of teenagers were now hunched over the reflective table. Warily, I walked over.

"Hey," I said, eyeing the bag of white powder between the kids. "Where'd you guys get that? I'm looking for a hookup."

One girl offered me the dollar bill. "Want some of this?"

"I'm looking for more of a long-term relationship," I said, hoping for the best. I hadn't haggled for drugs since an undercover stint as a rookie. "Can you help me out?"

"Indoor pool," the girl said. "Look for Toto. He's wearing pink boxer shorts with rainbow ducks on them."

THE INDOOR POOL was near the back of the house.

Strangely, it wasn't as full of drunk teenagers as I expected it to be. When I tried to step through the glass doors, a muscular eighteen-year-old boy in a tank top stopped me.

"Wait a second," he said. "You have to pass a sobriety test to come in here."

"You're kidding."

He shrugged. "Bryan's mom would be mad if some drunk girl hit her head and drowned in the pool, you know? House rules. Touch your index finger to the tip of your nose."

I did as asked. "I'm looking for Toto. Is he in the pool?"

"Yup. Jacuzzi. Okay, walk along that line there. One foot behind the other."

I did the walk, internally laughing at the fact I had to perform this for an eighteen-year-old wannabe cop when I'd never done it for a real officer in my life.

"You're good," said the wannabe. He gestured me inside. "Have fun. But not too much fun."

About twenty people lounged in the pool, sprawled across donut and unicorn shaped floaties, but only one person occupied the spa. I spotted the pink boxers through the roiling water.

"Um, Toto?"

He glanced up. Ugly bright-green sunglasses obscured half his face, though it was dark in the pool room. From the looks of his round face, he was no older than twenty. How he had access to so many drugs was a complete mystery. "Can I help you?"

I sat on the edge of the spa, careful not to dip my shoes in. "I heard someone hired you to pick up insulin. I need to know that person's name."

He tilted his sunglasses down to look at me. "Sorry, lady. I don't share client information."

"You don't understand. My son, Benji, is missing. He's diabetic. I think whoever hired you is the person who kidnapped—"

Toto snapped his fingers. "Not my business! I don't poke my nose where it doesn't belong. That gets people into trouble."

"Listen here, you little shit," I snarled. "If you know something about my son—"

Toto reached out and touched the tip of his finger to my tongue, catching me completely off guard. "You need to calm down, lady."

A tiny, tasteless piece of paper dissolved on my tongue. Furiously, I spit it out, but the feeling of something there lingered.

"What was that?" I demanded, spitting again. "What did you just give me?"

Toto laughed and rested his head against the lip of the spa. "Relax, honey. Totally pure LSD. In a few minutes, you'll have nothing to worry about."

15

"**Mom?**"

A haze of white light filled the room. Benji's face appeared above me, his eyebrows scrunched together in concern. But this Benji was older, in his mid-twenties, with a square jaw and intensity of expression that mirrored his father. His voice, however, remained that of a child.

"Benji?" I reached up and stroked his cheek, feeling stubble beneath my fingers. "You're so handsome."

A halo floated above Benji's dark curls as he smiled. I frowned, confused.

"Are you an angel?" I asked.

Mid-twenties Benji disappeared, but his childish laugh echoed through the hallways of the party house. I propped myself on my elbows and looked around. Everyone had gone. The house was quiet except for Benji's voice as he launched into a haunting rendition of Old MacDonald.

As I shoved myself to my feet, a palm tree sprang out of the floor and bumped into me. I stepped to my left to avoid it, but another palm tree grew rapidly beside me. Suddenly, the room was filled with palm trees, swaying in a breeze that was actually visible. It rippled through the room like quicksilver.

The more I looked around, the more I noticed things changing and morphing. The walls expanded and contracted, as if the house was breathing. The pool water flowed around my feet, cooling the hot skin between my toes. One of the palm trees had arms, and it strummed a ukulele while the other plants danced.

"Mom, follow me!"

I turned toward Benji's voice, losing my balance as I pivoted. It was hard to walk when the floor was made of pool water. I waded through the hallway and looked up the stairs, where a waterfall of red fruit punch cascaded from the second story. Benji, about four years old now, waved at me from the top of the steps.

"Come on, Mom!" he called happily, beckoning me up. "You have to see what's up here. It's so cool!"

Picking my feet up seemed like a gargantuan task. Each one weighed a good thirty pounds. When I looked down, huge gold coins stuck themselves to my bare skin. I plucked one from the top of my foot and squinted at it. Ophelia's profile was stamped into the metal.

"Is Ophelia president?" I wondered aloud. "When did the US get gold coins?"

"Mom, come on!" Benji called impatiently. "We're waiting for you!"

I dragged one foot from the floor and placed it on the first step. The coins ricocheted off, turned into iridescent butterflies, and flew away. With my next step, the coins turned into a flock of rainbow birds. As I made my way upstairs, my Cinderella skills expanded. Oddly-colored mice ran past my feet, as did a few rabbits. A cat made of vape pen smoke wound its way through my legs.

When I reached Benji, he vanished and reappeared at the end of the hallway. He waved me forward. "Come look, Mom! I made you something!"

His drawings, the scary ones of the tree demons, walked along the walls. As I passed, they opened their mouths and laughed, displaying rows of sharp teeth. The hallway seemed endless. My feet moved, but I grew no closer to Benji. A red door appeared in front of me. I reached for the handle...

And walked into the basement of the meth apartment building. Two little boys faced the damp, molding wall. They held each other's hands tightly. From the back, I could tell the one on the right was Benji. His tight curls were unmistakable. The other boy looked over his shoulder at me. Did I know his face?

The boy lifted Benji's shirt and pointed to the insulin pump attached to Benji's torso. The cartridge was empty.

Heart pounding, I walked forward and circled around until I could see Benji's face.

He was all bones. His skin sank against his skeleton, stretching out his eye sockets. His beautiful blue irises were gone, replaced with gaping black holes. "Mommy," he gasped. "I'm scared. I don't want to die."

"You aren't going to die," I tried to say, but the words wouldn't come out of my mouth.

The other boy pointed to a set of amateur lab equipment across the room. On a shiny, silver table sat a single dose of insulin. I ran toward it, but the floor slipped out from under my feet. I landed flat on my back, staring up at the ceiling.

Benji fell. I heard his bones crack.

The little boy stood over me and looked down.

"Boom," he said.

The basement exploded.

"Miss?"

Something cool and wet touched my face.

"Excuse me? Miss?"

I struggled to lift my heavy eyelids. Sunshine lay across my face like a warm, heavy cat. My entire body felt sluggish and slow, as if someone had let me sleep in a deep pit of thick mud. I let out a groan.

"Are you okay?" asked an unfamiliar voice.

The wet thing blotted my face again. As the smell

of bile reached my nose, the memories of last night flooded back to me. I batted away the damp cloth near my forehead and pushed myself up to my elbows.

"Whoa, easy there." A young boy, maybe a year or two older than Ophelia, sat back on his heels. He held a clean washcloth. "You have gum in your hair. I was trying to get it out for you."

I reached up and touched my scalp. Sure enough, a big wad of bubblegum was stuck to my bangs. "I don't remember chewing that."

"A lot of people won't remember last night."

I looked around at the carnage. The party house was full of teenagers in various states of hung over. They were draped over sofas and across the floor. A few even managed to fall asleep on the stairs. I returned my gaze to the sober boy with the washcloth.

"I know you," I said, studying his face.

He stared right back. "Yeah, you look familiar too. Are you friends with my mom or something?"

"What's your mom's name?"

"Kathleen."

"I don't know any Kathleens."

"Huh." He offered me the washcloth. "Don't take this the wrong way, but what's a nice lady like you doing at a house party for teenagers?"

I dabbed at the sticky gum, but water wasn't

going to do the trick. "I had some business to attend to."

"With Toto?"

"How do you figure that?"

He grimaced and rubbed the back of his head in second-hand embarrassment. "You were kind of the talk of the party last night."

I pushed myself into a sitting position. "What do you mean?"

"Do you really want to know?"

"Yes," I insisted. "Tell me."

The boy clicked his tongue. "Well, it started when you decided to hula dance in front of everyone in the living room. You said you were in Hawaii and kept shouting about palm trees."

I smacked my forehead. "Oh, God."

"Then you told everyone you were a special agent for the FBI," he continued, trying to contain a chuckle. "And that you were here to investigate the people at the party."

I held my tongue. Better this kid thought I was seriously tripping rather than have him know I was telling the truth.

"You kept pointing at random people and yelling 'You can't handle the truth!'" He laughed at his own impression. "It was pretty funny. Anyway, then you started talking about some guy named Amos. It seemed kinda private, so I took you to one of the bedrooms upstairs to ride it out."

"You did?" I asked suspiciously. "Why?"

The boy shrugged. "I mostly come to these parties to look after my friends, but you seemed like you needed help more than they did. First time on acid?"

"Second," I admitted. "I tried it once in college. Not really my thing."

"Mine either." The boy offered me his hand. "I'm Scott, by the way. You're Carolina, right?"

I took his hand, and he pulled me to my feet. "Did I tell you that last night?"

"Yeah. Special Agent Carolina Clark."

I rolled my eyes. "That's my ex-husband's last name."

"Oh, I know."

"What else did I tell you?" I said, scared of the answer.

"Not much."

"Liar."

He winced. "Okay, fine. You said you were worried that someone named Ophelia was going to run away from home and become a hooker. Then you started talking about how Pilar was prettier than you and annoyingly perfect."

"That's enough. I don't need to know anymore." I looked at my feet. "Thank God. They're normal."

Scott glanced down. "Your feet?"

"It's a long story."

"I can imagine." He grimaced apologetically. "Sorry about my friend. He's really into microdosing. I'm not sure that's a real thing though."

"Your friend?"

"Everyone calls him Toto. He told me he slipped you a tab of acid."

"The twenty-year-old in the hot tub. Right." I examined Scott's young face. "How does a kid like you get to know someone like Toto?"

Scott plucked a piece of sticky candy off the front of the sweatshirt I'd borrowed from Ophelia. "I met him on the slopes at Wolf Park a few years ago. He bought me a hot chocolate when my mom ditched me for some dude she thought was cute."

"Happy family life, huh?"

He managed a smirk. "We're all screwed up in some way or another. It's cool though. I live with my grandparents. My mom visits around this time of year to pretend she still loves me. Really, she just likes the free vacation. Grandpa pays for it."

That's when it clicked. As Scott smiled warmly, I realized why I'd recognized him: he was the boy from the pictures inside 3 Saint John Drive, Copper and Glinda Billings' grandson.

Did this teenaged boy know anything about Benji? I resisted the urge to bombard him with questions. So far, I'd escaped the consequences of breaking into an elderly couple's house. I couldn't give myself away now.

"So," I said, trying to sound casual. "Does Toto deliver?"

Scott scoffed. "Why? I thought last night was a fluke for you."

"It was," I replied. "I was wondering if he's ever been to your house."

"No way," Scott said. "Toto's not the kind of guy you give your address to."

"Do you know what his real name is?"

He took a step backward and crossed his arms. His entire demeanor shifted as he went on his guard. "Wait a second. Are you actually an FBI agent?"

"No," I said. Technically, that was true. I was retired from the agency. "But I did come here for a reason, and it would help if I knew Toto's real name."

"I'd like to help," Scott said. "But I owe too much to Toto to risk getting him in trouble. He's a good guy, just misguided sometimes. Plus, I'm not supposed to be here."

"Why not?"

He gestured to the plethora of unconscious teenagers. "Look at this place. This is the kind of house party you see in movies, not real life. The last time my grandparents caught me out all night, they grounded me for a month. They don't want me to turn out like my parents."

"I thought you were here to help your friends."

"Yeah, I am." He chewed on his bottom lip. "But I guess I like coming to parties too. By the way, are these yours?" He lifted my car keys from a cup of M&Ms. "No one else here drives a Chevy."

I took them. "Not all of us can afford beamers. Thanks for your help. Get home safely, okay?"

"You too. Sorry I couldn't tell you what you really wanted to hear." Scott walked me to the entryway and held the front door open for me. "See you around?"

"Probably not."

ONCE INSIDE THE MINIVAN, I peeled off Ophelia's sweatshirt. It was caked with melted candy and questionable biological material that smelled like strawberries and gasoline. I balled up the fabric and chucked it into the trunk, wanting it as far away from me as possible.

As the engine warmed up, I kept an eye on the big house. Scott hadn't left yet. Instead, he tended to the young teenagers waking up on the front lawn. He brought out cups of water, returned clothes and coats to their owners, and ushered his friends into

Ubers home. Why did one kid care so much about a group of entitled party-goers?

An hour later, Scott came out to the front porch and checked his watch. Hurriedly, he hopped on a bicycle that had been leaning against the house and pedaled down the driveway. When he rounded the corner, I put the van in drive and followed after him.

Slowly, so he wouldn't notice me creeping along behind him, I trailed Scott toward the front of the gated community. At each corner, I stopped to give him time to get ahead of me. His legs pumped furiously as he sped along. At the security checkpoint, he waved to the guard inside and zoomed off.

Meanwhile, I waited impatiently for the iron gate to swing open and let me out. At a glacial pace, the bars moved outward. As soon as the gap was wide enough for the minivan, I squeezed through it.

Scott and his bicycle had disappeared. I swore and banged the steering wheel. I closed my eyes and let instinct would take over.

"Left or right, Carolina?" I asked myself. "Just pick one."

On a whim, hoping some magical god was guiding me from above, I turned right. Unfamiliar with this route, I wasn't sure where to go next. The road curved through other neighborhoods. Scott could've cut through any one of them, but I kept driving straight.

At a four-way stop, I glanced left and caught sight of his dark green bicycle as he flew past an ugly orange house. Cutting off the car across from me, I made a sharp turn and hit the gas.

I caught up with Scott on a long straightaway. I stayed way back, afraid he might hear the engine rumbling behind him and glance over his shoulder at my van. His coat fluttered behind him as the wind ripped through his hair. He had to be freezing, but he didn't let up his breakneck pace.

I trailed him until the look of the neighborhoods changed. The houses grew smaller and less obnoxious. The cars were less expensive. My Chevy fit in with the other minivans and crossovers. As Scott wheeled up to a familiar house with white shutters framing the windows, I realized where he'd led me: back to his grandparents' place on Saint John Drive.

Scott leapt off his bike while it was still moving and walked it up to the porch. When the front door opened, he flinched. An older man—Copper Billings probably—came out on the porch, waving an angry finger in Scott's direction. I cracked my window, hoping to hear the conversation.

"Out all night again, Scotty?" Copper was saying. "What have we told you about that?"

"Sorry, Grandpa," Scott said, bowing his head. "But I wasn't doing drugs or anything. Brandon went to Bryce's house, and—"

"I don't want to hear any excuses," Copper interrupted. "Your grandmother has been worried sick. You know what it does to her when we don't know where you are."

"I left a note on the kitchen table."

Copper lightly batted Scott around the ears. "You left the house without permission. You know what that means."

"I'm grounded?"

"For at least a week," Copper confirmed. "Now go sort the recycling."

"Grandpa, it's freezing! Besides, trash day isn't until tomorrow."

"No excuses," Copper said. "You break the rules, you face the consequences. Get to it, boy." The older man's face softened as he looked over his grandson. He patted Scott's cheek. "We're hard on you because we worry about you. That's all. When you're done, Grandma has breakfast waiting for you." As he turned to go inside, he added, "Don't forget to put your bike away."

Scott wheeled the bike to the garage attached to the house and pulled the door open. He dragged two heavy-duty plastic bins to the curb, then began breaking down a pile of cardboard boxes. He shoved the flattened boxes into the bin, occasionally pausing to stomp on the pile. After ten minutes of solid work, he wiped his forehead and braced himself against his knees. As he heaved for breath, I leaned forward with a worried expression.

Scott fumbled for something in his coat pocket and pulled out a red inhaler. He puffed it once, then twice, before taking a deep, steadying breath. Then he went back to his recycling duties.

"Scott Turner," I muttered, finally remembering the name from when Mila had told it to me. "Who are you, and what do you have to do with my son?"

16

I sped back to the resort, intent on doing a deep dive into Scott Turner's life. Part of me felt crazy for suspecting a boy who looked no older than fourteen or fifteen, but there had to be a reason for all these coincidences. Scott's missing inhaler, his connection to Toto, and his grandparents' address on the ransom letter meant something. I just had to figure out what.

As I pulled into the long driveway that led up to the resort, the security guard stopped me at the gate. I rolled down my window.

"I'm staying here," I said.

"We're checking everyone's ID," the security guy replied. Behind the tinted windows of the gatehouse, a police officer from Petra's division watched our interaction. "Wolf Park PD's looking for someone."

"Aubrey Wharton, I know." I showed him my driver's license. "I'm the one Detective Lee is working for."

The security guard studied my license and handed it back carelessly. "Sure, ma'am. You can go on in. Parking lot A is full though. You'll have to park in overflow. Make the first left."

"That's quite the walk," I commented.

He shrugged. "It's not so bad. People walk from the restaurants there all the time."

"And disappear from them," I muttered under my breath as I drove off.

The overflow parking was right next to the restaurant we'd taken Benji for his birthday. The heartbreaking moment between Amos and Benji felt old and stale, as if it had happened years ago. Somehow, it was like Benji had been gone forever, and I'd grown old and weary during my search for him.

Starting at the restaurant, I retraced our steps from that night. I played the events over in my head: Benji's disappointment over Amos's forgetfulness, the sad way he'd asked to be excused, the minute or two I'd taken to yell at Amos when I should have been following Benji to make sure he got back to the room safely.

I remembered seeing Benji walk past the window of the restaurant, but once we got outside, he had already disappeared from the path. His footsteps would have vanished too, but I was too frustrated with Amos's behavior to notice the warning signs that my son was gone.

Slowly, I walked the path to the resort, sweeping my gaze back and forth. The trees swayed gently in the breeze, their branches bowing under the weight of the snow that rested there. The sky was blue, but it wouldn't be for long if the weather report was right; Wolf Park was expecting another few inches of snow during the night. In the distance, above the secluded cabins that were still under construction, storm clouds gathered.

As I passed the spot in the trees where we'd figured Benji had been taken, I stopped and took a deep breath. Cold air shuddered out of my lungs, and my chest heaved with pre-sobbing spasms. I hurried onward. If I was going to lose it, I should get out of the public view.

I ducked my head and pushed past a happy family heading out early. The little girl, maybe five or six years old, slipped on something on the path. Her dad caught her before she fell and gave her a reassuring smile when her lips almost parted to cry. As the family walked on, my eyes widened at the sight of the item that had caused the girl to slip.

It was a drawing.

I swooped to pick it up and held it up to my eyes. This time, I recognized Benji's hurried scrawl right away. The lines were drawn the same way, and the picture featured the same scary figure with bent legs. On the horizontal part of the legs, Benji had drawn a strange triangular logo. He had also added a rough sketch of what looked like one of the cabins on the slope, but a torn flag, outlined in black, rose from the chimney.

Hope blossomed in the pit of my stomach, but doubt threatened to quash it. Instinct told me Benji was leaving these drawings for me to find. At least he was alive, but if he had the opportunity to drop clues in my path, why hadn't he managed to let me or the police know where he was yet? I hung on to the idea that he was still alive and well enough to draw. Besides, I had one more day before I had to pay the ransom.

"Carolina!" a sharp voice cut through the cool air.

I looked up and saw Mila striding through me. From the sharpness of her gaze and the way her fists were balled up at her sides, I could tell she was pissed.

"Look what I just found," I said, holding up the drawing. "It's from Benji. He's leaving clues for me to find. He must be close by—"

Mila snatched the drawing out of my hand. "What the hell did you do?"

"What do you mean?"

"Aubrey Wharton fled the state," she informed

me, whisking her long hair over one shoulder. "Someone tipped her off that we were looking for her."

I shrugged. "So? It could have been anyone."

"And yet I have a strange feeling that you somehow managed to talk to her." Mila crossed her arms and studied me from head to toe. "I know you're working on this case by yourself. It's so obvious. What are you hiding from me?"

"I was trying to show you." I reached for the drawing, but she held it away. "Benji's here. He left that for me to find."

With a lifted nose, she examined the scrap of paper. "We'll get back to this in a minute. How the hell did you track down Aubrey Wharton before we did?"

"You forget I used to be one of the best special agents the FBI had ever seen."

"That's rich," she said. "Considering you gave it all up when things got tough."

"That hurts."

"Tell me about the maid."

I poked my tongue into my cheek, trying to stay my temper. "I followed some clues to a snowboarders' party. She happened to be there. I got what I needed from her. You don't need to detain her anymore."

Mila threw up her hands with a groan. Inhaling

deeply, she said, "What made you think you could take this into your own hands? You let a criminal get away."

"The only reason you wanted her was because of Benji," I reminded Mila. "Her life as a petty criminal doesn't concern the FBI."

"It doesn't matter," she shouted, drawing the attention of several passers-by. "We needed her! God, I'm trying to find *your* son, Carolina. Why do you keep getting in my way?"

I jabbed her chest. "Because you're not doing your job! I've made more progress finding Benji in the last three days than you and Petra have for the last two weeks. I guess we know why you never got that promotion you were gearing for at the agency. You don't have the skills for it."

Mila lifted her hands. I braced myself for the flat-palmed push we had been taught to create space in difficult situations, but it never came. Mila spun on her heel and stalked away.

"Don't do anything stupid," she spat over her shoulder. "Or I guess I should say don't do anything *else* stupid."

Without Mila on my side, I was truly alone. I gave her a head start back to the resort then followed after her, my footprints landing in hers. Benji's drawing kept me moving forward. If he was drawing, he was alive. I kept repeating that fact to myself. It was all that mattered.

After a quick visit to the cafeteria to load up on enough food to satisfy me for the rest of the day, I locked myself in my room on the second floor and logged onto my laptop.

Scott Turner, like every other teenager in existence, loved social media. The only trouble I had locating his online presence was separating him from the multiple other Scott Turners in the world. Once I found his Instagram account, his SnapChat, Twitter, and TikTok popped up in related searches.

As I scrolled through his content, I learned a few things about Scott Turner. He was a sophomore at Wolf Park High School, where he ran track and competed with the debate club. However, film seemed to be his true passion. Most of his posts featured short snippets of random video clips—his friends boarding, the sun setting, a close up of two people holding hands—edited together with a cool song in the background. He never mentioned his parents on any account, but his grandparents got a few shoutouts. It looked like they had done the majority work of raising him.

I scrolled past the first few pages of search results for Scott Turner, looking deeper into the web. Most of it was random bullshit, and I almost zoomed right past the piece of information that would change everything. Quickly, I scrolled back up to take a second look.

A headline screamed at me: *Four-year-old boy abducted by his father, rescued from meth lab in apartment building.*

I clicked on the link but got a 404 error. I growled in frustration, hit the back button, and read the blurb below the link on the search page: *After months of searching, the FBI located Scott Turner, the four-year-old boy who stole America's heart when he was reported missing. The kidnapper? The boy's own father...*

The blurb ended there, but I didn't need to read the rest. I knew everything about four-year-old Scott Turner, because I was the one who had found him in that damned apartment building.

I leaned back in my chair and rubbed my eyes. No wonder that kid had been haunting my dreams, LSD-laced or not. No wonder his name had sounded familiar each time I'd heard it. For the months when Scott was missing during his childhood, I'd lived and breathed that name. But like everything else that happened at the agency, I'd blocked it from my memory when Amos and I had gotten divorced.

But why had he turned up now? What were the odds that a kid I'd rescued in the past would cross paths with me again over ten years later? And what did any of it have to do with Benji?

I dialed Mila's number on my phone, but it rang

and rang until I got sent to voicemail. Three additional calls later, I gave up and rode the elevator up to her floor. With a heavy fist, I banged on the door to her suite.

"What?" she demanded when she finally answered. A sneer crossed her face when she saw it was me. "Oh, good. Are you ready for round two?"

I bullied my way past her and into the room. "I need you to access an old case file for me."

Her jaw dropped in disbelief. "Are you crazy? Get out. I'm mad at you."

"I don't care if you're mad at me," I said. "I need you to look this up. Do you remember Scott Turner?"

"The kid with the inhaler?"

"Yes and no." I showed her a picture I'd found on the Internet, the same picture of four-year-old Scott Turner that had circled around the nation on every major news outlet when he had gone missing all those years ago. "This Scott Turner."

Mila's eyes widened. "I know that kid! We pulled him from a meth lab. That was one of the first jobs I worked with you."

"You wanted to know what I was hiding, right?" I took the ransom letter from my pocket, unfolded it, and handed it to her. "I got that two days ago. Scott lives at that address."

"You think Scott kidnapped Benji?" she asked.

"That doesn't seem right. What would a teenaged boy want with your son?"

"I don't think it was Scott," I said. "I talked to him. He seems like a great kid who got dealt shitty parents. But there is a connection between him and Benji. I'm sure of it, but I need the damn case file to figure it out. Can you get it for me or not?"

Mila bit her bottom lip. "This is illegal, Carolina."

"I've been doing a lot of illegal things," I admitted. "I don't care if Petra ends up arresting me. Just make her wait until after I find Benji. Please, Mila. Do this for me. Do it for Benji."

Mila fiddled with her phone. "I'll make the call. In the meantime, go back to your room and wait there. Don't cause any more trouble, or the deal's off."

"You got it." I gave her a hug. "Thank you."

"Get off me," she said, half-heartedly shoving me away. "I'm still mad at you."

Swiftly, I planted a kiss on her cheek and left her to her own devices.

17

Unable to wait patiently, I paced my tiny room in anticipation of Mila's call. I kept the curtains open and watched the path outside. I didn't expect to see Benji come along and drop another drawing, but I could always hope. Hope kept me moving forward.

After half an hour, I could have sworn I'd worn a path in the old carpet beneath my feet. It was starting to look duller than the rest of the room. Chewing on my nails, I forced myself to sit in the armchair by the window. My leg bounced. I couldn't contain the anxiety in my chest, and the pills waiting for me at the pharmacy weren't going to help. I needed my son back.

At long last, my phone buzzed. I knocked over a

lamp in my haste to reach it. The bulb hit the floor and burst as I greedily answered.

"Hello, Mila?"

"No, it's your mother."

I bristled, irritated. "Mom, I'm waiting for a very important call, so whatever this is about—"

"Ophelia skipped school today."

My breath whooshed out of my lungs. No, this could not be happening. I needed at least one child safe at home. "Where is she?"

"Oh, I've got her," my mother said, and my pulse settled itself. "Found her at the skate park around the corner from the house. What should I do with her? My plan was to smack her upside the head until she admitted what she'd done wrong, but I understand corporal punishment isn't all the rage these days."

"Did you ask her why she skipped class?"

"She's been silent since I found her."

"Put her on the phone."

I tapped impatiently on the windowsill as the phone switched hands. On the path below, I spotted Petra and two of her other officers marching toward the lobby. What were they up to?

"Mom?"

"Hey, O," I said. "What's going on?"

"Nothing," she muttered.

"Why'd you skip school?"

She blew a sigh. "When are you coming home?"

"Answer the question, O."

"I didn't want to be there."

Petra and her cohorts disappeared from my view. Suspicion crept up my scalp. Something irked me about the detective.

"O, you have to go to school," I said. "It's important."

"Why? Benji isn't in school."

"He's going to have a lot of work to make up when he gets home," I said. "You won't be jealous of him."

"What if he doesn't come home?"

I swallowed the lump in my throat. "O, don't think like that. I'm going to find Benji."

"Yeah, right."

"Listen to me," I said in a serious tone. "Don't give up, do you understand? You *cannot* give up, because that's when things go sideways. Always push forward. Keep hoping. Remind yourself that things are going to get better."

Ophelia's voice grew thick. "What's the point?"

"The point is to live," I replied. "You are alive, O. Make the most of it. Experience things. Be the best you can be. You're only young once, and when you get older, you'll regret not appreciating these years more."

"Are you in a competition to tell me as many cliches as possible?"

I snorted. "I'll do better when I get home, I promise. In the meantime, I need you to stay safe. Listen to Grandma. She's trying to take care of you."

"She keeps making soup. I hate soup."

"Ask her to make something else."

"I can do that?"

I rolled my eyes. "Yes. She's not the best at reading nonverbal cues. You have to tell her."

"Oh, okay. I'll try that." She paused. "Hey, Mom?"

"Yes, honey."

No answer came, but I heard Ophelia's breath hitch.

"It's okay, baby," I said, trying to keep my voice steady. "Everything's going to be okay." My phone buzzed again. I glanced at the screen and saw Mila's number. "O, I'm getting another call that I have to take. It's about your brother. I love you. Mwah!"

"Bye, Mom. Love you."

With a broken heart, I switched calls. "Hey, Mila. What do you got for me?"

"Answer your door, idiot."

I peered through the peephole and saw Mila standing on the other side of it, lip curled upward in annoyance. I pulled open the door and hung up.

"Here," she said, holding out a chunky laptop. "The file you want is on there, but you need my computer to access it. The password's on a sticky note, which you need to burn once you type it in. If you tell anyone I did this for you, I'll kill you myself. And believe me, no one will ever find the body."

I accepted the laptop. It must have weighed twenty pounds. "Ugh, I don't miss lugging this thing around. Do you wanna come in?"

"Hell no," she said flatly. "Besides, I have a meeting with Petra."

"Have fun."

"Don't tell me what to do."

I almost followed her when she stalked off, determined to get her to like me again, but the weight of the laptop reminded me that I had a job to do. After I found Benji, I would apologize to Mila and make things right.

As I set the laptop on the desk and lifted it open, it felt like no time had passed since I'd left the agency. This was just another case, another missing child that I had to find. I logged in using Mila's credentials then held a lit match to the sticky note with the password. As the small piece of paper crumpled in flame, I dropped it into the bathroom sink and ran the water so the smoke alarm wouldn't go off.

Once inside Mila's account, I clicked the link she had left for me. It led me straight to the files for Scott Turner's case, and it included everything from the grandparents' initial interviews to the final review of Scott's mental and physical health once we located him. I skimmed through the contents as quickly as possible, relying on the case details to fill in the blanks of my shoddy memory.

Copper and Glinda Billings had one daughter, Kathleen, who married Michael Turner when she was freshly twenty-two. Not long after, they gave birth to Scott. A year later, both Kathleen and Michael were charged with child abandonment and reckless endangerment, and Scott's care was transferred to his grandparents.

The first thing I noticed was that Scott's parents had not been interviewed after his disappearance. Neither one of them had been accounted for at the time of Scott's disappearance, which was a huge red flag. It automatically put both of them on the suspect list, especially since neither one of them had custody over Scott. My team had put a lot of effort in tracking them down. Eventually, we found Kathleen in a rehab center, where she had admitted herself under a fake name to avoid social embarrassment. After extensive questioning and gathering statements from witnesses, we discovered she had been in the rehab center during the time of Scott's abduction.

Tracking down Michael was a different story. He had a habit of flying under the radar, even before his son disappeared. According to the grandparents, he was a good-for-nothing drug addict who would do anything to get enough money for another hit, including marrying Kathleen for her modest inheritance. Before they met, Kathleen was the perfect girl next door. She went to church and participated in community plays. Michael's influence, said the Billings, steered her the wrong way. In addition, Scott's existence came down to Michael's manipulative abuse.

She didn't want his baby, Copper Billings wrote in a statement to the agency. *He kept pressing her to get pregnant, but she wasn't ready. He replaced her birth control with sugar pills, and she got pregnant with Scott. She's Christian, so she refused to get an abortion. Michael led her to believe her pregnancy was an act of God. My wife and I think he did it to keep her around. She struggled to stay clean throughout her pregnancy, with no help from him. When Scott was born, he was never around. It was only after we got custody that he started pretending to care about his son.*

UNTITLED

I sat back and stretched, processing everything I'd read on the case file. The details came back to me in a jumble of jagged pieces, but I couldn't put the puzzle together. I squeezed my eyes shut and tried to remember the last time I'd seen Michael Turner.

It was in court. He would go to prison for abducting his own son and holding him in an apartment full of meth. Scott had been treated at the hospital for methamphetamine withdrawal, as the drug had the unhappy ability to seep through the skin. Michael Turner, from what I recalled, was under the impression he'd done nothing wrong.

"You took my son from me!" he hollered from the witness stand.

He was as thin as a rail, with sunken cheeks and ruined teeth from all the drugs he'd done. His eyes bulged from their sockets as he screamed at me. The second-hand suit he wore hung limply from his shriveled shoulders. His lawyer tried to hush him to no avail while the judge's eyelids fluttered with boredom.

"This is your fault, you heinous bitch!"

I said nothing, crossing one leg over the other as Michael Turner signed his own prison sentence. His outburst proved one thing: he was guilty.

I pinched the bridge of my nose to hold in my emotions. I'd watched triumphantly as Michael made a fool of himself in court. Looking back, I recognized the situation for how sad it was. Michael was an addict with mental health issues. If society addressed the root of the problem, hundreds of kids like Scott could be spared the same childhood trauma, and people like Michael wouldn't end up in prison for things they had limited control over.

But what about Benji? He had two sober parents. Sure, we were divorced, but we had intentionally done our best to keep the kids out of it. The reason he was gone still remained a mystery.

Frustrated, I started pacing again. I spotted Benji's drawing sticking out of my coat pocket and took it out to examine it again: the cabin, the creepy man, and his long bent legs with the triangular mark on them. What did it mean?

I glanced outside. A couple attempted holding hands and carrying their skis at the same time as they walked toward the slope. The girl dropped hers, and the skis slid across the icy sidewalk. The guy ran after them, laughing as he picked them up and handed them back to her. As the skis rotated, I caught a glimpse of the logo on the bottom of each one: a little triangular mark.

Heart pounding, I lifted Benji's drawing. The man's legs weren't bent at an odd angle like I'd originally thought; he was wearing skis. A memory flashed in my head.

A good-looking man with hazel eyes and blond hair caught my eye in the window's reflection. He came over and gestured to Benji, who played in the snow outside.

"Is he yours?"

"Yup." I pointed to Ophelia, snowboarding on the rails. "That gremlin belongs to me too."

"You're lucky," replied the man. "My wife has my son for the holidays. I won't see him until next year."

"Sorry to hear that."

He shrugged. "Divorced life, you know?"

I laughed drily. "Oh, I know. We're here with my ex-husband, his new wife, and her two daughters."

"Wow, that's rough." He smiled, displaying nice even teeth, and stretched out his hand. "I'm Michael, by the way."

I jolted back to the present with a violent gasp. My breath caught in my chest and swelled like a balloon.

Pain blossomed in my lungs. I fell off my chair, onto my hands and knees, as light exploded in front of my eyes. I hyperventilated, unable to calm myself long enough to slow my breathing.

I crawled into the bathroom, grabbed a towel, and pressed it over my nose and mouth. The thick fabric forced me to inhale and exhale at a reasonable pace. A minute passed, then two. Gradually, the panic attack passed.

Someone pounded on the door, nearly launching me into another round of hysteria. I forced myself to my feet, left the bathroom, and pressed my eye to the peep hole.

Petra waited on the other side, with six officers behind her. I backed away from the door. This was not good.

Petra knocked again. "Carolina, I know you're in there! Answer the door!"

I did not obey. Instead, I crossed the room and threw open the window. A gust of cold wind blew my hair back as I judged the drop to the ground.

"Kick it in," Petra ordered one of her officers.

A heart-stopping thud echoed from the other side of the room as someone launched their boot at the door. The lock held, but it wouldn't stay that way for long.

Twenty feet down. I'd be lucky if I didn't break a

leg, but my choices were dwindling. I sat on the frame and swung my legs outside.

The door fell with a resounding crash, and Petra's officers rushed in, guns at the ready.

I leapt off the window sill.

18

I landed in a thicket of decorative holly bushes that bordered the edge of the resort. On the upside, they broke my fall. On the downside, the prickly leaves scratched and tore at my hands and face as I dropped into the branches. Worse still, my left wrist whacked against the brick building. I suppressed a yell of pain as my bone crunched. It was definitely broken.

Cradling my hand to my chest, I looked up. Petra hung her head out of the window and spotted me in the bushes below.

"Don't you dare move," she hollered. "You're under arrest!"

Channeling Ophelia's chaotic vibes, I laughed and rolled out of the bushes. Something about directly disobeying Petra's command gave me the power I needed to compartmentalize the pain in my wrist and sprint off in the direction of the slopes. Was this how Ophelia felt when she broke the rules or skipped school? I was starting to understand the thrill of it.

"Get back here!" Petra screamed.

I shoved past the tourists and ran up the path. I had no idea where I was going, but I had to get away from Petra and her sycophants. My car wasn't an option. It was too far away, and Petra could set up a barricade within minutes to stop me from leaving the area. Besides, leaving Wolf Park was the last thing I wanted to do. I had to find Michael Turner. If I found him, I strongly suspected that I would find Benji.

Someone sturdy stepped into my path, and I ran smack into Mila. She grabbed me by the arms to keep me from slipping on the ice.

"Mila, let me go," I gasped. When was the last time I ran like this? "Petra—"

To my utter shock, Mila spun me around and pushed me into a sprint. As she ran alongside me, she said, "Petra found out what you did. She knows you broke into the Billings house and tracked Aubrey Wharton at that party. I can't believe you broke into someone's house!"

"I didn't think they'd find out," I huffed, pumping

my arms for extra speed. "Are you on my side again?"

Barely missing a breath, Mila replied, "I'm always on your side, even when I'm pissed at you because you're acting crazy. Turn left and head uphill. I know a place."

I leapt off the trail and fought my way through the deep snow. When we reached the thick trees that bordered the resort, I headed up the slope. Thankfully, the massive branches kept too much snow from coating the ground. It was easier to navigate the uneven ground without having to worry about slipping on ice.

My lungs burned as we climbed higher, but I forced out a question. "Does Petra know you're helping me?"

"No, are you kidding? She'd have me arrested too. I can't afford that."

"Why are you doing this?"

"Because I don't want my best friend to end up in prison for the rest of her life," she replied, finally losing her breath as she stumbled over a gnarly tree root. "Besides, Benji and Ophelia need you. Now shut up and keep moving."

I was more than happy to oblige, since I didn't have the stamina to talk anymore. We delved deeper into the forest, moving westward, until I could no longer see the ski trails at Wolf Park. The sky grew dark, and as the sun abandoned us, the chill set into my fingers and toes.

"How much farther?" I gasped.

"We're getting close. Over that ledge."

I stared up at a huge piece of rock jutting out of the side of the slope. "You've got to be kidding me. You expect me to climb that? Do I look like Bear Grylls to you?"

"Shut up," Mila grunted. She laced her fingers together to form a small platform. "I'll hoist you."

I stepped into her hands and reached for the rock ledge. With a groan of effort, she heaved me upward. I grabbed the rock and pulled myself the rest of the way up. My shoulders creaked and popped. As I rolled to safety, I let out a soft moan.

"Ooh, that did not feel great."

"Hello?" Mila said from below. "I kinda need a hand."

Laying on my stomach, I dangled my hand over the edge. Mila grabbed my wrist with both hands and yanked herself up like a professional rock climber. She sat next to me to catch her breath.

"Where the hell are we going?" I asked. "Am I going to freeze to death before we get there?"

She pointed toward a dark structure about a hundred yards away. "We're here."

It was an old cabin, built way before Wolf Park Ski Resort had ever been erected. From the looks of its dilapidated roof and crumbling stone walls, no one had lived there for a long time.

The front door was rusted shut, so Mila and I shouldered it open together. The cabin's interior had weathered the snow and storms rather well. It didn't smell of mold, though some rat droppings in the corner indicated the local animals had found the place before we did.

"How did you know this was here?" I asked.

"I studied maps of Wolf Park on the way here." She wandered over to the fireplace, stacked a few logs, and brought a lighter out of her pocket to get a flame started. "I plan a safe house for every mission, just in case I need one."

"That's smart," I admitted. "I never thought to do that."

A small flame crackled and sizzled. Mila ripped up old newspapers and fed it to the fire until it began to grow. I knelt by the hearth and warmed my frozen hands.

Mila shook off her coat, revealing the backpack she was wearing beneath it. She shrugged it off her shoulders and set it next to me. "Food and water to last a few days. Hopefully, you won't need it for that long."

As she headed for the door, I shot to my feet.

"Where are you going?" I asked.

"To lead Petra in the wrong direction," she

replied. "You need time to come up with a plan, don't you?"

"To find Benji?"

"To get out of this mess you made," Mila corrected. "I can't vouch for you, Carolina. You need to clean this up yourself. I'm just giving you some time to figure it out." She blew out a long breath. "I'll be back in the morning to check on you. Don't leave or freeze to death."

"I'll do my best."

Once she was gone, the cabin grew quiet except for the wind that whistled overhead and rattled the windows. I pulled off my wet socks and let the fire warm my feet before checking the backpack.

Mila had left me two big canteens of water, several cans of microwavable soup, and a box of saltine crackers. In the cabin's small kitchen, I found a tin sauce pan. I wiped out the dust and used it to heat the soup, holding it precariously over the fire with an oven mitt.

As I ate lukewarm chicken and noodles, I checked my phone. The service up here wasn't great, but I had one tiny bar that allowed me to access the local news. I clicked on a thumbnail of a reporter standing in front of the ski resort, and a livestream began to play.

"We are currently broadcasting from Wolf Park Ski Resort," the reporter was saying. She was wrapped up in a coat and earmuffs, but her bright red nose and watering eyes gave away her discomfort. "Where detectives and officers from our local police department are on the hunt for Carolina Caccia, a woman rumored to have kidnapped her own son."

"Are you shitting me?" I muttered devilishly. "What are you up to, Petra?"

"Caccia's young son Benjamin reportedly disappeared from the resort approximately two weeks ago," the reporter went on. "Though Caccia claims to be innocent, she has broken several laws over the last few days, putting our Wolf Park officials on edge. I have Detective Petra Lee with me to give you more details. What else can you tell us about Carolina Caccia, Detective?"

I rolled my eyes as Petra stepped into frame. The reporter held the microphone near the detective's mouth.

"Caccia is mentally disturbed," Petra said cockily. "We are worried that she may cause harm to her son or other people. If you see her, do not approach her. Inform an officer immediately."

The reporter pulled the mic back. "Should we be concerned about having a criminal on the loose in Wolf Park?"

"My officers are here to find Caccia and keep you and your family safe." Petra stared emotionlessly into the camera. "Keep a calm head and go about your vacation, but report any suspicious activity you see."

Behind Petra and the reporter, police officers in full gear swarmed the slope and the resort. If that many guys had turned up to look for Benji on the first night he'd gone missing, maybe we would have had a better chance at finding him. Now, they were after me.

With an annoyed huff, I turned off the livestream and set my phone aside to preserve the battery life. I couldn't look for Benji now. For one thing, Petra's officers would find me in a pinch. For another, it was freezing. Despite my layers of clothing, I couldn't weather the mountain at nighttime.

I found a dusty blanket and curled up by the fire. Within minutes, my exhaustion carried me to sleep.

MILA KEPT her promise and returned at sunrise with a take-out container of oatmeal. Though it was nearly cold and I hated oatmeal, I scarfed it down, happy for something to eat other than canned noodles and vegetables.

"She's not backing down," Mila informed me of Petra's inane search. "I can't get her to lift the warrant for your arrest. If you leave this cabin, you're going to prison."

"I have to leave," I said between bites. "I have to find Benji."

She lifted an eyebrow. "How are you feeling?"

"Fine. Why?"

"Did you ever pick up the medication I ordered from the pharmacy for you?"

"No, I never got the chance," I said. "But I'm feeling way better than the other day. I think all the digestive issues and sweating were stress-related."

"Mm-hmm." She wasn't buying it. "So what's your plan anyway?"

"My plan hasn't changed. I'm going to find Benji."

She hummed impatiently. "Carolina, you have no leads—"

"I know who took him."

"Who?"

"Michael Turner."

Mila scrunched her nose. "Scott Turner's father? What does he have to do with any of this? He doesn't even live in the area."

"But his son does," I reminded her. "And he's always been obsessed with getting his son back. Remember at his trial? When he shouted that he lost Scott because of me? Well, I think taking Benji was his way of getting revenge. I think he was stalking his own son, and—"

"Stop," Mila said. "Just stop. Can you hear yourself talking, Carolina? You sound insane."

"He was *here*, Mila," I insisted. "Two weeks ago, while I was in the cafeteria, he walked right up to me and introduced himself. I didn't recognize him. He looks completely different now, not so drug-addled, but I know it was him! I even pointed Benji out to him." I took Benji's drawing out of my pocket and smoothed it out. "Look at the logo—"

Mila groaned. "Not this again. Anyone could have dropped those drawings—"

"I know it was Benji," I said. When she fixed me with a bored stared, I added, "This is not how I taught you to investigate, Mila. The facts are staring you in the face, and you still can't entertain the idea of the truth." I pointed to the roughly sketched cabin that Benji had drawn. "We need to find this place. I'm guessing it's one of the cabins under construction on the north side of the resort. I checked the local records. Construction is on hold until the snow melts. It's the perfect place to hold Benji until—"

"I'm not letting you out of here," Mila said. "You're paranoid, Carolina, and you're grasping at straws. I get it. You think you have to do whatever it takes to get Benji back, but entertaining these crazy ideas aren't going to help."

I growled in frustration and got to my feet. "You can't keep me here."

Mila stood and moved into my path before I could reach the door. "I can and I will. Face it, I'm in better shape than you. I saw you huffing and puffing on the way up this hill."

I tried barreling past her, but she swiftly set her shoulders and slammed into me. Stars exploded in front of my eyes as she wrapped her arms around me and tackled me to the floor. Pinned down, I struggled to heave her off me, but she had the advantage.

"I told you," she said. "You're not leaving."

She rolled off me and held out her hand to help me to my feet. I glared and smacked her hand away. She shrugged, sat on the decrepit sofa, and trained her eyes on me.

"I can do this all day," she said.

Momentarily defeated, I lay on the cold floor and stared at the peeling paint on the ceiling. Somehow, I had to get out of here. Benji was counting on me.

19

*A*s the day wore on and Mila thwarted every attempt of mine to escape the measly cabin, my agitation grew. I'd received the ransom letter three days ago. Tonight, if I didn't drop half a million dollars at 3 Saint John Drive, Michael Turner would do something unspeakable to Benji. I had to shake Mila, but I didn't know how.

The opportunity came after the sun went down and the fire grew low. As the cold crept in, Mila's eyes drifted shut. After a full day of restraining me, she was worn out. I forced myself to stay awake as she sank deeper into the moldy sofa, hands tucked in her armpits to stay warm.

Her chin dropped toward her chest. Her breathing deepened. When I was sure she was asleep, I wrapped the old blanket around her shoulders and put another log on the fire so she would stay warm. Then I got ready to leave.

I put on every single layer of clothing that I had. To preserve more warmth, I balled up the old newspaper pages and shoved them inside my coat for extra insulation. I swapped my gloves for Mila's since hers were lined with heat-generating fabric. In a dresser in the spare bedroom, I found two extra pairs of socks that hadn't been eaten by mice and pulled those on. From Mila's bag, I found hand-warmers. I activated four of them and slid one into each of my pockets and socks. At the bottom of Mila's bag, a pocket knife shimmered. After a beat of hesitation, I took that too. Then I laced up my boots, put on my hat, and braced myself for the cold outside.

The two challenges from the day before still remained. The cold was brutal at night on the mountain, and Petra and her gang of police officers were still out there searching for me. I walked to the edge of the rock face and gazed across the valley. The lights of Wolf Park shone in the distance. Dark spots along the white mountain gave away the placement of the half-constructed cabins. If I squinted, I could make out police lights near the road. Oh, well. It was a chance I'd have to take.

I sat on the edge of the rock face and slid off the end. Fortunately, my snow pants took the brunt of the damage as I slid down the steep incline and landed in the knee-high snow below. I covered my face with my scarf and plowed through the trees, the thought of Benji propelling me forward.

Every so often, I scrambled a few feet up a tree to check my bearings and make sure I was heading in the right direction. After an hour of hiking, the unfinished cabins finally came into view. Petra's team hadn't made it up this way. Perhaps she thought I wouldn't consider hiding out there.

Another challenge arose: there were at least thirty cabins along the slope, and the path between hadn't been cleared of snow. I had no idea which one Michael might have been hiding Benji in.

Once more, I took out Benji's drawing. The paper had softened from how often I'd been handling it. The lines, too, were less pronounced, but I could still make out the details. The cabin Benji had drawn matched the ones below. The porch was only half-built, but everything else seemed finished. One thing separated Benji's drawing from the real cabin: the little flag he'd drawn flying near the chimney.

I squinted across the dark landscape, wishing the moon were a bit brighter as I studied each cabin. Each one looked identical to the last, until—finally—I spotted it: a white rag tied to a metal stake meant to support the chimney while the cement was still drying. My heart jumped into my throat.

"I'm coming, baby," I whispered.

The descent to the cabins was steep. I half-hiked, half-fell through the snow, letting gravity do most of the work for me. Hidden rocks and branches scraped my knees, but I quickly made it to the first row of cabins. They had been built in sets of four, and the one with the flag was about two and a half sets away. While the other cabins were dark, the flicker of a fire burned in the one I'd singled out.

I darted from cabin to cabin, keeping to the shadows. If Michael saw me before I could get to Benji, it would mean trouble for everyone, but it was hard to move quickly through the deep snow. After an excruciating dash across an open stretch, I ducked into the darkness behind the flagged cabin. Slowly, carefully, I peeked through the window and into the main room.

My chest almost burst with relief, and I clapped a hand over my mouth to stifle my sob. There was Benji, pale white and shaking but alive. He was secured to a wooden chair with zip ties. The plastic bit into his wrists and ankles, leaving angry red welts. At the moment, he dozed fitfully, his head lolling on his shoulders.

I scanned the room for any sign of Michael. Empty liquor bottles were piled up near the door. Fast food wrappers littered the floor. But there were no coats or boots to indicate that Michael was at the cabin. Taking a chance, I knocked softly on the window.

Benji shook himself awake and craned his neck in search of the sound. When his blue eyes met mine, my chin trembled. I waved.

"Mom," he said silently. His eyes filled with tears.

I put my finger to my lips and mouthed, "Is Michael here?"

He shook his head.

I glanced down the path to make sure it was clear then tried the door. It was locked from the inside. "Damn it."

Benji threw me his saddest puppy dog eyes.

"Don't worry," I said, hoping he could read my lips through the window. "I'll be back."

Near the adjacent cabin, a workman had left a heavy axe. I picked it up and slung it over my shoulder. When I approached the window, I motioned for Benji to turn his head away. When he obeyed, I slung the axe toward the window with all of my might. The heavy metal head shattered the glass.

I used the axe to clear as many shards as possible then tossed the tool aside. Carefully, with my hands inside my coat sleeves to protect them, I shimmied through the window and into the cabin.

"Mom!" Benji cried.

I threw myself around him, hugging him tightly. I touched his cheeks and traced his jawline, as if to convince myself he was actually there. Fat tears rolled down his face as he laughed.

"I knew you'd find me," he said.

I went to work on the zip ties that held him to the chair, using the pocket knife I'd swiped from Mila's bag. "You helped a lot. How did you manage to get your drawings all the way to the main resort area?"

"I snuck out," he declared proudly. His shoulders and smile dropped quickly, though. "Just long enough to slip the second drawing into some skier's pocket. I didn't think you would find it."

I freed his hands. "And you paid a girl to get your insulin?"

"Yeah, Michael brought a computer in here," Benji explained. "When he left, I used it to hire Aubrey. She was nice."

"Baby, why didn't you have her call the police?"

Benji's lip wobbled and moisture built in his eyes again. "I couldn't. He said he would hurt you and Ophelia if I tried to escape or tell anyone I was here. Mama, he's crazy. He's always drinking, and his eyes get all crazy sometimes. All black and bloodshot."

I cut through the zip ties around his ankles. When he was free, I cradled him to my chest. "He's an addict, baby. He's probably using drugs too. Where is he now?"

Benji sniffled and wiped his nose. "I don't know.

He said he had to go do something. Can we go before he comes back?"

"Yes," I said, taking his hand. "Let's go. Careful of the glass. Don't cut yourself."

We stepped cautiously over the broken window and toward the door. As I reached for the handle, it turned on its own. The door swung open, and Michael Turner stood framed against the snowy backdrop.

His pupils were almost as large as his irises. He grinned wildly. All the charm he'd employed in the cafeteria a couple weeks ago was gone. The chaos in his expression robbed him of his good looks. His blond hair was tousled, and he hadn't shaved since I'd last seen him. His sweet smile, I knew, was fake.

"You fixed your teeth," I said. "When we first met, you had meth mouth."

He stepped over the threshold, and I shoved Benji behind me.

"So you finally figured it out, huh?" Michael said. "You know who I am?"

"Michael Turner," I breathed. "Guilty of abducting your own son. Guess I caught you twice now."

"Twice?" Michale's empty laugh echoed through the cabin. "Honey, you never caught me the first time. Your little team of agents did all the work. Now it's just you and me."

Benji trembled behind me, his fists tightening as he twisted his fingers around the fabric of my shirt.

"Why are you doing this?" I asked, trying to stay calm. "I did you a favor. I kept your son safe. If he'd stayed in that apartment, he'd probably be dead by now."

Michael roared, spittle spraying from his mouth. "You robbed me of the only person I ever loved!" He slammed his fist against the wall, leaving an ugly indentation. "Scott was my son, and you took him from me! It's your fault I've gone ten years having to watch him from afar while the damned *Billings* raised him! And his mother—" Michael gasped and paced to the other side of the cabin. "That horrible bitch. She shows up once a year and pretends like she cares about him. *I* should be the one who has access to him, but no! They took out a restraining order on me!"

"You've been stalking your son, haven't you?" I asked. "That's why you're in Wolf Park. That's how you ended up seeing me at the resort. You were there because you knew Scott would be too."

Michael's chest heaved as he caught his breath. "It shouldn't have to be like this."

"I agree," I said simply. "But you brought this on yourself. If you had gotten help earlier—"

His rage returned as quickly as a gasoline fire. "Don't put this on me. This is your fault!" When he took another step toward us, I shifted sideways and kept Benji behind me. His eyes narrowed as he zeroed in on me. "I wanted you to know what it felt like to lose a child. I wanted you to feel the fear I felt when I thought I'd never see Scott again."

"Mission accomplished," I said. "Now let us pass."

He sneered. "You think it's that easy? You think the last ten years have been easy for me?"

"I imagine not."

"You imagined right." He stalked toward us. "Kidnapping your son wasn't good enough for me. The real revenge is taking Mommy away and letting her kids think she abandoned them. You have a daughter, right? How devastated will you be when she realizes you're never coming home?"

I bit my lip so hard that it began to bleed, but I gave no other indication that Michael's threat had affected me.

"Would you like to watch the tears stream down her face?" he asked in a low growl as he advanced further. "I'll show you."

I tracked his every step, and when he lunged, I was ready for it. I ducked aside, taking Benji with me, and stuck out my foot. Michael's boot caught around my calf, and his own momentum sent him flying toward the broken window. I clasped my hand against the back of his neck and helped his head meet the sharp shards of glass lining the window sill.

Benji gasped as Michael flopped to the floor, his face a mess of bloody cuts and scrapes. The force of his fall had knocked him unconscious, but I knew from experience that he wouldn't stay that way for long.

"Don't look," I advised Benji, taking him by the hand and pulling him toward the unlocked door. "It's time to go."

Leaving Michael behind, I carried Benji to freedom.

20

ONE YEAR LATER

"Don't run! Hey, are you deaf? I said don't run!"

I sighed as Ophelia and Marin sprinted past me and bumped into an elderly couple at the Wolf Park Ski Resort check-in desk. The couple's bags tumbled over.

"Sorry!" the girls chorused. Together, they righted the fallen suitcases before running off again.

"Hey!" I called after them.

Someone chuckled behind me. "Some things never change. Do they?"

"Pilar!" I gave her a big hug. "I feel like I haven't seen you in so long."

She kissed my cheek. "Well, this mysterious new job of yours keeps cutting into our Friday night dinners. I'd be offended if I didn't have Ophelia and Benji to keep me in the loop."

"I promise, I will tell you everything at dinner tonight," I said. "I've just had so much stuff going on. Where's Amos and Nessa?"

"Nessa found Benji outside," Pilar replied. "They're looking at boobies."

"I'm sorry. What?"

"Boobies," Pilar repeated.

"Yeah, no. I heard you the first time, but I need some clarification."

She tipped her head back and laughed. "Apparently, it's some kind of new bird Benji's obsessed with. He's showing the pictures he took of them when you all went to the beach this summer."

"Oh!" I said. "That's a relief."

"And Amos is bringing in the bags," Pilar added. She looked over his shoulder. "There they are."

Nessa and Benji bounded through the double sliding doors. Benji's camera swung from Nessa's neck as she happily hugged me around the waist.

"Hi, Lina!" she said.

"Hi, Mom!" Benji said.

The two ran off to join Marin and Ophelia. The girls were plucking quarters out of the fountain water and pocketing the change. I rolled my eyes.

Amos arrived next, rolling a suitcase in each hand and carrying the girls' duffel bags over one shoulder. He'd cut his hair so close to his scalp that his curls were no more.

"Hey, pack mule," I teased. "Good to see you."

He purposely set the duffel bags on my toe as he leaned down to kiss my cheek. "Can't say the same for you. Those kids are already corrupting the girls."

"Amos!" Marin shouted, holding up a handful of quarters. "I got five bucks! I won the bet!"

Amos gave her a thumbs up as Pilar crossed her arms and fixed her husband with a hard stare.

"What bet?" she asked.

He cleared his throat and avoided eye contact. "Nothing. Should we check in?"

"Amos," she warned.

He rolled his eyes. "I bet her she couldn't find more than five dollars in the fountain, okay? She was jabbering my ear off. What was I supposed to do?"

"Good Lord," Pilar said, strolling off to check her family in.

Amos put his arm around me and squeezed. "How's it going, Lina? The kids say you're working on some top-secret project. Is it true you quit teaching at the college?"

I wrapped my arm comfortably around his waist. In the last year, our friendship had repaired itself, and physical touch no longer felt like a boon. "Yup. I hated teaching anyway. I always preferred doing."

"And what are you going to be doing?" he asked.

"I'll tell you at dinner. It's a surprise."

"Hmm. What about this boyfriend of yours?"

I lifted an eyebrow. "How do you know about Parker?"

"I'll give you one guess."

"Ophelia," I grumbled. "Kid can't keep her mouth shut."

Amos grinned. "So how come Parker didn't come on vacation too?"

"We've only been dating a few months," I said. "I didn't want to confuse the kids. I want to make sure it sticks, you know?"

"How'd you meet him?"

"PTA."

He gaped. "You're in the PTA?"

I shrugged. "I'm trying to be more involved at school. You should talk, Mister Soccer Coach. Ophelia says you're harder on her than everyone else on the team."

"What can I say, I want her to be better than everyone else," he replied. "If she plays through high school, she could get a scholarship to college. By the way, I need to meet this Parker guy. Gotta make sure he's good enough for you."

"We'll see."

. . .

THE GIRL IN THE SNOW

AFTER CHECKING IN, all seven of us headed to one of the newly-completed cabins. It had four bedrooms, three bathrooms, a kitchen, and enough living space for all of us to enjoy our vacation without feeling like we'd be standing on top of each other the entire time. Ophelia and Marin happily shared a room, as did Benji and Nessa. Since Parker wasn't here, I got my very own king-sized bed, all to myself.

When dinnertime rolled around, we walked to the restaurant together. I gave our name and reservation details to the hostess, who seated us at a table for nine.

"Wait a minute," Benji said, glancing at the extra chairs. "Who else is coming?"

"Surprise!" sang a familiar voice.

Benji and Ophelia sprang to their feet, nearly knocking Mila over with affection as she came into the room.

"Mila!" Ophelia said. "What are you doing here?"

"Your mom will explain in a second. Do you guys remember Rosie?"

Mila's daughter—younger than Benji—waved shyly from behind her mother. At once, Benji and Nessa pulled one of the empty chairs between them for Rosie to sit down in. Mila moved the other empty chair next to mine.

"So?" Amos prompted, settling at the head of the

table. "What do you have to tell us? Are the two of you getting married?"

Pilar elbowed her husband in the ribs.

"What?" he grunted. "They'd make a great couple."

"We're not getting married," Mila said. She turned to me. "Want to do the honors?"

I beamed around the table. "Mila and I are going into business together."

A stunned silence filled the room.

Amos leaned forward. "That's why you quit your job?"

"Yup."

He looked at Mila. "And why you retired from the agency?"

"Yup," she replied.

"We've been working on getting our private investigator licenses," I explained. "Then we created an LLC. We'll be up and running by next week. Gotta start building a case load."

"Wow," Amos said, grinning. "Color me impressed."

"I think it's a great idea," Pilar added. "This way, you get to make your own schedule. You won't have to rely on the agency for anything."

Mila unfolded her napkin and set it in her lap. "That's a challenge as much as it is a blessing. Without the agency to back us, we'll have to make our own connections and gather our own resources."

"We can do it," I assured her. "Don't worry."

"What kind of cases will you be working on?" Pilar asked. "Missing children?"

"We can't afford to be picky," Mila explained. "We'll take whatever cases come our way."

"The world is our oyster," I said.

"What about your criminal record?" Amos asked me in a teasing tone.

I shot him a wry look. "You know it got scrubbed when we found Benji. My record is clean."

The server arrived. "Good evening, everyone. My name is John. I'll be taking care of you tonight. Can I get you started with some beverages?"

"Shirley Temple!" Benji crowed.

"Excuse me, sir?" I said pointedly.

Benji bowed his head. "May I have a Shirley Temple, please?"

John chortled and jotted Benji's order on his notepad. "Yes, you may. Next?"

I smiled at my family as they ordered their drinks. The struggles of the past few years—my jealousy of Pilar, arguing with Amos over the kids—were long forgotten. By some miracle, we had formed one big unit. The kids got along, and Amos had made an effort to spend more time with Ophelia and Benji. Pilar was teaching me how to cook, and my business with Mila was ready to take off. Everything was falling into place.

Mila leaned into me. "You okay?"

I smiled back. "I'm the best I've been in a long time."

Made in the USA
Monee, IL
27 February 2022